To my son, Noah. You're always my muse.

The Passenger

Jacqueline Druga

ONE

It was a good crowd and had remained that way throughout most of the show. The venue was small, and the lively group of individuals made the place look packed.

The size of the crowd surprised Jonas Truett, considering the no-name bar was located on a back road in the middle of nowhere.

How they got the gig was a fluke. The owner caught their video online. The basement studio recording of Jonas and the guys covering a seventies' tune had less than three hundred views. Yet, the owner saw it, loved it and invited them to play. Live music was a dying art. Jonas had been playing guitar since he was a teenager. Having the chance for their full band to play, instead of doing just some acoustic act, was an opportunity they didn't want to pass up. Even if it was two-hundred miles from home.

Surprisingly, the show for the most part was a success.

The loud cheering and screaming had Jonas Truett feeling like a rock star when he broke into his guitar solo, the second to last song of the third set.

Then the fight broke out.

Some local guy wound up tight, calling Jonas some hot shot making moves on his girl.

Jonas could have let it go. Nodded it off with a, "Yeah, yeah, man, whatever."

But Jonas was a hot head and anger begets anger.

Words were thrown with chest to chest pushes, and Jonas took a hard right to his cheek before the fight was stopped.

The local guy calmed and offered he and Jonas do the grade school, 'shake hands and make up' thing.

Jonas refused, insisting the guy be removed.

This didn't help Jonas' mood though. That guy got the first and last punch, and Jonas felt like a tool. Fueling a pouting, stomping behavior Jonas often demonstrated when he got ticked off.

He wished he could blame his reaction on copious amounts of alcohol, typically it was to blame and made it worse. But Jonas stopped drinking hours earlier. Not because he wanted to, but because the hotel was ten miles away and he had to drive some winding road just to get to the highway.

Being drunk in unfamiliar territory wasn't a good idea. However, a six pack to go was.

The fight took the wind out of the band's sail, bringing the fervor down several notches, especially when the crowd trickled away during their last set.

The end of the night couldn't come fast enough for Jonas.

Finally, it did. The bar was empty except for a few stragglers who probably closed the place every night.

The band members just wanted to leave, come back and tear down the big stuff the next day. However, Jonas didn't want to leave his gear behind.

Brett, the drummer stood on the stage, finishing the last of his beer, and grabbed his stick bag. "You want me to wait for you?"

Jonas wrapped his cords. He rolled them in neat loops so they wouldn't get tangled, then set them inside the small, canvas gym bag. "Nah, I'm good, thanks," Jonas replied. "If I don't see you tonight. I'll see you in the morning."

"Sounds good." Brett took a step off the edge of the stage and stopped. "Whoa, hey ..." He bent down and lifted something from the floor. "Is this your phone?" He held it up.

Jonas glanced over with a slight squint. "Yeah. Was it on the floor?"

"Yep. Probably knocked off in the fight." He extended it to

Jonas.

"Tell me before I look, is the screen broken?"

Brett examined the phone. "Nope. But you have four missed texts from your mom."

"I saw them, I just didn't open them. Thanks." Jonas grumbled and took the phone. He gazed down at the phone, still not opening the messages. He didn't need to. They were short texts. The last one probably came in during the fight.

Hey, let me know you got there okay.

Have a good show, love you.

Are you okay?

Please let me know you're okay.

After putting his phone in the front pocket of his gear bag, Jonas pulled a cloth from his open case and lifted his guitar from the stand. He should have put it away first. He didn't, he wasn't thinking as clearly as he should have. He still stewed about the events of the night, how things went from a mega high to a bad low.

He loved his guitar and lifted it with care. The design on the body of the custom made instrument looked like cheese curls. Jonas was inspired when he saw one that looked like ramen noodles. The guitar stood out and it sounded great. It didn't look quite as awesome when it was smudged, so Jonas polished the finish after every gig, before putting it back in his case.

"Hey," a male voice called out to him.

Jonas turned and his eyes cast down to the glass placed on the corner of his amp. A shot's worth of dark liquid in the rocks glass. "Don't put that there." He told the man.

"It's for you."

"Nah, thanks, though."

"Come on," the guy said. "A peace offering. Sorry my friend decked you."

"I'll pass, but thanks."

"Don't be a jerk."

Only because Jonas didn't want to get into another confrontation, he took the drink. It was just a shot, and Jonas' tolerance to alcohol was pretty good. That shot wouldn't do anything. He lifted it to the guy, "Appreciate it," Jonas said, then downed it. He lowered the glass to the floor and the guy took it.

"I got it. Good show. Nice guitar." The man pointed, turned and walked away. He waved to the few remaining patrons at the bar before leaving.

To Jonas, it felt like a strange encounter, then again, the entire night had gone off the rails. He finished packing up his stuff. He folded his guitar stand, tucked it under his arm and lifted his amp.

He carried them from the stage, calling out to the bartender that he'd be back in for that six pack.

The old beater car he had borrowed for the gig was parked in a spot in the lot not far from the building. Only three other cars remained, and they were near the door. He put his amp and the stand into the back seat then returned to the bar.

He walked straight to the stage, grabbed his guitar case and it was when he lifted and shouldered his gear bag he felt it.

A tingling ran across his forehead and a quick dizziness hit him as if he stood up too fast. Shaking it off like a cat, Jonas walked to the bar where he saw the brown bag waiting for him.

He set down his guitar case so he could reach for his wallet, but his fingers stumbled, and he dropped his wallet to the floor. Bending down to get it, he swayed some.

The woman bartender asked, "Are you okay?"

"Um, yeah, I just got dizzy for a sec."

"Are you alright to drive?"

"Yeah, I had like one shot in the last three hours," Jonas replied as he opened his wallet. Suddenly there were two wallets, his fingers fumbled for the debit card before he slid it to her. He blinked several times to clear the double vision.

"Are you sure?" she asked. "Maybe you should call for a ride."

"Nah, I'm. I haven't eaten all day. The hotel isn't far."

That was it. The food factor. Jonas could feel his stomach twitching and his hand shook. The bartender handed him the card and a slip with pen. Jonas scribbled a tip and his signature, placing the card back in his wallet.

After saying, "Goodnight." He grabbed his bag of beer and haphazardly tried to shove his wallet back in his rear pocket, so much so it dropped right from his pocket to the ground the moment he walked out the door.

TWO

Cate Truett had a connection with her son. With both her children actually, but mainly her son. Most mothers have it. A gut feeling, a worry that creeps up letting her know of something happening. A fine-tuned mother's instinct that was a blessing at times, and at other times not so much.

No one could deny Cate's instinct, not even Jonas, even though he tried. It was there, and sadly, it tended to only kick in where there was a problem or trouble.

Unfortunately, with Jonas for the past several years it was constant.

When he was a boy, of course, she worried. Normal stuff. How did he do with studies, with other kids in school, would he look both ways before he crossed the street?

The bumps, the bruises, broken bones and stitches, all the trips to the emergency room were Jonas being a boy. Where his sister Jess rarely caused worry, Jonas made up for that. Yet, it wasn't anything major, nothing that would foretell of things to come.

Cate remembered her grandmother telling her, "When they are little, they break your things. When they're grown up, they break your heart."

And that was nothing short of the truth.

When he was little, despite his misgivings, he was a good kid, he would never do anything to hurt anyone. However, somewhere along the lines of his life, when he was old enough to know better, Jonas decided he didn't want to follow those rules any longer.

How? Why?

Maybe Cate missed the signs, viewed her children so much through rose-colored glasses she didn't see it coming. How could the boy who would never say a mean word or hurt anyone, suddenly stand up his high school sweetheart turned wife, on their anniversary, and take off with some girl he met at Subway days earlier? Because she 'got' him, connected with him.

No one could have predicted that.

Well, almost no one.

Jessie did.

She told her mother Jonas hadn't been happy for a while, that he married, got a responsible job too early in life.

Hurting others was no excuse.

No excuse for the path he decided to take. He was fired from his job as a music teacher, left his wife, dropped the clean cut look and transformed into something emotionally, mentally and physically unrecognizable.

Cate had known her son to have a beer here or there, and never did she know him to do drugs.

His 'flip of the switch' change was something she never would have expected.

He played in two or three bands, stayed wherever he could, drank day and night, slept very little, ate less and fueled his lifestyle with a destructive cocaine habit.

A drug habit, Cate found out, that started before he left his wife.

He had spent all their money, lost his job over it, and he just … didn't care.

Cate did. He was her son and she loved him.

Every time he was in a fight, arrested, or found in some sort of 'rage' episode, Jonas would swear he was done. Finished. Over.

Cate would say the same. Never again. Tough love.

Then he would get in trouble again, call Cate and say, "Mom, I need you."

She would be there.

Every time he said he wanted help, Cate and her husband, Grant, would do what they could.

They exhausted what they could of Grant's 401K, took a loan against the house, set him up with the best rehabs, only to have him leave days later.

Jonas was addicted to the lifestyle as much as he was the drugs and alcohol.

Eventually, Jonas stopped the drugs, more than likely because he couldn't afford it. He still drank and behaved badly.

There were moments of hope, a spark of the Jonas he used to be would emerge and he'd go through a spell of staying out of trouble. He'd pay his fines, stay in line … only to fall again.

She joined support groups and the other women in those groups, the mothers, they understood, they were the same way. Overly worried, anxious.

It scarred Cate, made her grayer than she should have been.

It made her neurotic and despise those mother instincts because they were right most of the time. She always knew when a call would come about Jonas. Just like she did on this night.

Something was wrong.

It started with a twinge in her stomach early on.

She dismissed it at first, it was a weekend, she always worried about Jonas on the weekends.

Then she justified her worry was he was going out of town for a gig. He was fine, she was just overreacting again.

She searched her gut for an answer and every time she reasoned herself into a calm state, something would set her off.

The last time was a car insurance commercial.

She wasn't good company for Grant and couldn't focus enough on the movie. She told him they started watching it too late, she was tired and was going to bed.

Cate did go to bed. Just not to sleep.

With a heavy sigh, back propped against pillows in bed, she set down her book and reached for her phone on the nightstand.

Nothing.

She opened up her messages and he hadn't even read her texts.

Her fingers hovered over the phone debating on sending one

more text when the bedroom door opened.

Grant stepped in and paused. "I ... thought you were going to sleep."

"I said I was going to bed. How was the movie?"

"Good, you should have watched it." He walked over to the bed, pulling down his side of the covers. "What are you doing?"

"Do you think Jonas is alright?"

"Yes." Grant climbed into bed.

"But he hasn't read my texts or replied."

"He had a gig."

"I know but ..."

"Cate."

"I was thinking of texting Jess to see if she heard from him."

"Stop."

"Grant, I'm worried," Cate said.

"You're always worried."

"But I feel it. I do." Cate ran her hand on her stomach. "I have this gnawing feeling. This horrible doomed feeling."

"You really need to stop. It's all the time. Cate, he's fine. You need to learn how to let things go."

"He's our son."

"He's a grown man," Grant said. "We may not like how he lives or what he does, but it's not for us to say. You drive yourself crazy, not to mention me and Jess about this."

"You know ... you know I pray so much and so hard for him that I swear God is probably tired of hearing it."

"That's not how that works and you know it. Maybe you're just not hearing the answer. Go to sleep. It's late."

Cate leaned back, staring at her phone. "I'm not going to be able to. I know I'll be looking at this thing all night. Waiting for it to ring. I feel it, Grant. I just ..."

"Okay, alright, stop." Grant slipped from bed. "Give me the phone."

"What? No."

"Cate, I mean it, give me the phone. I'm going to take it downstairs, put it on the charger there and make you a cup of chamomile."

"What if it rings and he needs us?"

"Then he'll call my phone." Grant held out his hand. "I can't have you do this to yourself. Because, Cate, no matter what happens, you can't control the outcome."

"You're right." Cate placed the phone in his hand. And she knew he was right; she just didn't say the words. She couldn't control things, and some days she accepted it, but tonight was not one of those days.

She knew he was concerned, too. He didn't say it. He didn't have to. His actions spoke louder than words when he took the phone, walked to the door and paused to look at it before stepping out.

THREE

Things turned fuzzy fast for Jonas. Not even a blast of early summer, cool air helped when he walked out the door. A weird pressure built on his forehead and it seemed like his surroundings moved every time he shifted his eyes.

His feet scuffed against the gravel of the parking lot as he made his way to his car. The back door was open from when he put his amp in there. He didn't even remember leaving it open.

The way he felt, Jonas would have sworn he was drunk. But he was far too much of a professional drinker and knew he hadn't consumed enough booze to get him to that state.

It had to be something medical.

He was coming down with something.

He put the guitar and gear bag into the back seat, closed the door, and keys in hand, dropped in with a sloppy slide into the driver's seat.

He pulled the door shut and jumped from his skin when he saw the man in the passenger seat.

"You're in the wrong car," Jonas said.

"No. I'm not," he replied.

The man looked tired, around the same age as Jonas, his hair shoulder length and dark. He wore a gray shirt, a uniform or something, and he was already buckled in.

"You're not with that guy, are you? Like here to try to kill me or beat me up?" Jonas asked.

"What guy?"

"The guy I got kicked out for doing this." Jonas pointed to his bruised cheek.

"Ah, no. I'm not with anyone from in there."

"What do you want?" Jonas asked.

"A ride. I thought I'd take this ride with you."

Jonas' head swayed as he put the key in the ignition. "To the hotel?"

"To wherever."

"What's your name?"

"You can call me David," he replied.

"I'm Jonas."

It was surreal, almost dreamlike, a part of Jonas wanted to tell the guy, "Dude or David, if that's your real name, get out of my car." But he didn't.

He wasn't feeling well, he was off, and Jonas thought it best, stranger or not, to have someone in the car with him.

He started the ignition, buckled up and pulled from the parking lot.

The road seemed even more winding than when Jonas first had driven to the bar. It was dark, now he was nervous. His hand gripped and released the wheel, sweat formed on his forehead and the car felt like it was floating. Everything was floating.

Two miles.

Two miles until the next road, Jonas told himself.

He knew he was driving slowly; he would have driven that way even if he felt fine.

It was as if he held his breath the whole ride on the snake-like road, even pausing for a second before turning on to the road that would lead to the highway.

"Are you alright?" David asked.

"Um ... yeah. Just still mad about tonight."

"And you're still mad about the fight?"

"Just everything. It was a good night, we sounded great. I'm in the band."

"I saw the guitar."

Jonas nodded. "Yeah, we uh, were uh ..." He stammered his words, slowed down to a crawl until he saw the exit for the highway.

"You were what?"

Think, Jonas, think. Keep talking to this guy. The hotel isn't that far. Almost there.

"We were playing great. The crowd loved us, and this guy just brought it all down."

"How?"

"By fighting with me. Picking a fight. Getting me mad."

"So, he picked a fight with you, you got mad, it escalated into a physical fight, and it was him who ruined the night?"

"Yeah."

"Don't you think you could have turned the other cheek?" David suggested.

"I did and he punched it."

David chuckled. "I'm pretty sure that's not how it went."

"Were you there?"

"I've been there. I'm in this car because of it. Look," David said "Our actions and reactions cause outcomes. They may not be the outcomes we may have wanted or imagined. Denying it isn't the answer. Admitting the truth is the first step to righting a wrong and to setting you on a new path."

Jonas blinked hard, his eyes felt heavy and David's words suddenly had an echo.

"Are you all right?"

Jonas shook his head. "I'm not drunk, I swear, I didn't drink enough. I feel like it though."

"Why don't you pull over and let me take the wheel?"

"I think I—"

"Jonas! Deer!"

Crash.

The animal was a blur as it slammed onto the hood of the car then into the driver's side of the windshield. Even in his best state, Jonas wouldn't have had time to react. Then again, had he been in a good state, he would have seen that deer.

The instinct to hit the brakes came too late, Jonas pushed his foot down to the peddle and jerked the wheel.

The car slammed into something else. It was a hard hit, jolting his head against the driver's window.

He didn't know what it was he hit nor was there time to think about it. It was violent, sending the car into a three-sixty tailspin before slamming again and flipping the car.

That was when it seemed to happen in slow motion.

Jonas had zero control as the car rolled. He felt the shattered glass hit against his face like a hard rain, and visions of his parents flashed before his eyes as the car stopped rolling and turned upside down, it then sailed airborne over the embankment.

A calm feeling overcame him, his body went limp and he thought, '*This is it. Nothing I can do.*'

There was no bracing for impact, he didn't know when that would occur. It didn't matter anyhow. Thoughts of his family suddenly were blurry, then gone as the car crashed down hard, roof first.

For a single split second, Jonas felt it and then ... blackness.

FOUR

It sounded like someone dropped something, a loud bang, that jolted Grant awake after he finally started drifting into sleep. He knew there wasn't a sound, he didn't hear anything. Grant was well aware of the sensation. It was a hypnagogic sound. Usually, he had them when he was stressed and decided to read something intense. It didn't happen often, typically it was a voice or music. He learned the term when he first started teaching history at the community college. Thankfully, the older he got, the less it happened. He should have expected it on this night.

Cate stressing made him feel stress; he just didn't show it.

The tea worked on her. Although it didn't ease her mind. Grant could tell by the way she slept. On her side, one hand rolled to a fist just under her cheek, the other clutching the covers as if she expected to wake and fling them off at any moment.

His eBook reader had slid down from his chest. He was glad he didn't fling it across the room when he sat up. Grant preferred the feel of a book in his hands, but being in his late fifties, even glasses at night didn't make those tiny words any bigger or brighter.

After placing his reader on the nightstand, Grant slowly got out of bed so as not to wake Cate. He slid into his slippers and made his way across the bedroom. He was thirsty and he could get a drink of water from the bathroom, but Grant wanted juice.

In the dark kitchen he grabbed a glass and opened the fridge. He poured some into the glass, drank it quickly, then poured some more. That was when he saw Cate's phone on the counter connected to the charger.

Bringing the glass to his lips, he reached down and touched the screen.

No new messages.

Jonas hadn't replied.

A lump formed in his stomach; one he had felt before. It caused instant nausea. Grant had to tell himself to stop, just stop. Jonas was a grown man. He was fine.

Even though he thought he couldn't help but worry just a tad and feel bad about the last time he talked to his son, or rather, argued with him.

It happened not long before he left for his gig.

"No," Grant told Jonas, as they stood in the driveway right outside the house. "No."

"Are you serious?" Jonas hissed. "You're not letting me borrow your truck?"

"No, Jonas, I'm not."

"I have a gig."

"I know."

"It's three hours away."

"I know," Grant said.

"I walked all the way over here for your truck, you told me I could take it," Jonas barked. "You think maybe you could have told me before I walked here that I couldn't. I talked to you on the phone."

"And on the phone, I couldn't smell the alcohol on your breath."

Jonas huffed. "Oh, come on, it was one beer. I'm not drunk."

Grant tried to stay calm and reasonable. "The last time I lent you my truck for a gig, you told me you got drunk."

"And I said I was sorry."

"I know." Grant nodded. "You promised me, you promised you wouldn't drink and drive."

"It was one beer."

"It's still drinking and driving."

"You're ridiculous."

"No, you're ridiculous, Jonas. It's two in the afternoon."

Jonas flung out his hand and stepped back. "I'm done."

"Wait, how about this," Grant spoke, walking to his son. "Why don't I take you? I'd love to see you play. Maybe I can get up and jam with you guys. We'll make a guys' weekend out of it. What do you say?"

Jonas laughed. "I don't want you there, Dad. I don't want you up on stage."

"Then ... then I won't go. I'll only drive you."

"Forget about it."

"Jonas, you have to go to your gig."

"Oh, I'm going." Jonas stepped away.

"How are you going to get there?'

"Don't worry about it."

"Jonas ..."

"I said," he spat angrily. "Don't worry about it. I'm not your problem anymore."

It was a tough love card Grant didn't like playing. He wavered a little but held tight. Now, he regretted it some. Finishing his juice, Grant started to go back to bed and stopped.

Maybe he was worrying too much or Cate was getting into his head, but Grant lifted her phone and immediately dialed Jonas.

He expected his son to answer the phone with irritation, what he didn't expect was for it to go directly to voicemail.

He stared for a second at the phone but didn't leave a message.

It was after three in the morning, more than likely Jonas' phone was dead.

He was fine.

He felt a brief flutter of concern, but Grant tucked it away and went to bed.

FIVE

He knew he was in some sort of accident, but Jonas just didn't know how or why it happened. He tried to think, but it was a blank. He didn't feel any pain, none at all, maybe it was the shock. The only discomfort he had was when he blinked his eyes. He could feel the shards of glass across his lashes.

The car was upside down and Jonas was on his stomach, out of his seat. His belt was undone, he didn't even remember unlocking it. His first awareness after the accident was this moment.

He could feel his eyes getting heavy and a strange pressure in his head. His vision blurred some. He could smell something. Was something burning? Fuel? He didn't know. But Jonas was aware he had to get out of the car. The busted windshield would be his exit.

He could feel himself fading, but he knew he had to fight it.

Preparing to belly crawl out of the car, it hit him.

The man that got in the car with him.

Unless he was remembering wrong, there was a man.

Jonas couldn't recall his name. Dan, Devon, David … It was something like that.

Was he all right? Hurt?

Quickly, Jonas turned his head to the passenger seat.

It was empty.

Fading …

Where did he go? Did he get out? The door wasn't open.

Jonas didn't assume the man crawled out, his first assumption was he was thrown, and Jonas panicked.

Thinking, 'I have to get out. I have to get out', Jonas reached forward and lifted his chest.

Fading....

Blackness.

A sensational burning pain in his temple and instant head-ache caused Jonas to grunt loudly and open his eyes.

Now he was on his back, outside in the grass. He rolled to his side, wincing as another pain shot through his ribs. The wrecked car was twenty feet from him. He could see the small amount of dancing flames coming from where the engine would be. They were blue, not orange.

How did he get to the grass?

He only vaguely remembered being in the car. It was as if he had just woken up from a dream, one that faded quickly. He knew he wasn't thrown because he knew he was in the car prior to passing out, he felt it, but he couldn't recall climbing out.

He felt lucid now, aware, every moment before that was snuffing out fast.

One memory stayed strong.

The man in the car.

What was his name? What was his name? Jonas repeated in his mind.

David.

That was it.

It hurt so much to stand, but Jonas did. First to his knees, then using the slanted ground, he crawled until he was straight.

"David!" he yelled out. "Dave ..." He cringed and grabbed his side.

Was he in the car? Jonas couldn't remember if he saw the man still in the car. If he was, Jonas had to get him out. After all, how long would it be before the car would be totally engulfed in flames?

He staggered a few steps and felt lightheaded. The closer he walked to the car, the more of a tunnel vision it appeared.

His knees buckled ... he took a step ...

Black again.

Jonas' eyes opened fast to the loud sound of a truck going by.

Awake again.

Aware again.

The sound was close, too close, it vibrated against his chest as he lay on his stomach. He could feel a mixture of grass and gravel under his hand and a strong heat against his legs. Looking at his hand, Jonas noticed the orange glow. He rolled to his back and instantly panicked.

He was on an embankment, down the grade a good hundred feet was his car. It blazed wildly, smoke billowing up, flames sparking and shooting high.

Utter fear swept over Jonas in that instant. His body trembled and he was truly scared. There he was alone, on that hill, injured.

He felt tremendously hopeless.

It wasn't dying that scared him, it was dying on that hillside and never being found. What it would do to his parents.

"Help!" He cried out, his voice barely making a dent in the dead of the night, he released a single sob and called out again. "Help."

He looked around, hoping to see the man that was in his car, but he couldn't see him.

Jonas cycled quickly through panic, fear and sadness, then just a fast as it hit him, it was gone.

He didn't know why he felt sad, where it came from. In fact, everything he had just felt was fuzzy. He was fading in and out of awareness. It was coming in waves, lucid moments that made the minutes before hazy and dreamlike.

Breathing heavily, and really unaware fully of what he was doing, he crawled the rest of the way up that embankment.

He made it to the guardrail and used the metal barrier to stand. The moon was bright. Bright enough to give some illumination to the highway so he didn't have to wade in a sea of dark.

Jonas tried to climb over it, but barely had the strength.

He rolled over the guardrail and onto the berm of the road with a grunt.

Stand up, he thought. *Stand up. You need help.*

Using the guardrail again, he lifted to a stand. He was discombobulated, looking around.

Not a car in sight.

As he turned to his left, there it was, a good distance, barely seen, a mere speck in the road, but he knew it was a deer that lay there. It was by a bent up guard rail. Was that his accident? How did he get so far away?

Jonas started to stagger, going back and forth between the side of the road and the blacktop of the highway.

He didn't have direction. Jonas knew he just had to keep moving, but his body felt otherwise.

It gave out on him.

His legs wouldn't move. He tried with everything he had to keep walking, keep standing, but he stumbled out into the road. He knew it wasn't a good place to be. Actually, it was the worst place his failing body could be.

But Jonas didn't have a choice. He felt like he just folded. Collapsing down, dropping to his knees on to the highway.

He wasn't able to move. He tried, but he couldn't, even when he saw the headlights of the car speeding his way.

He knew it was the end and braced for that split second when it would all be over.

SIX

Russ McKibben was a good man, everyone knew it. Hard when he had to be, soft when he needed to be. He had been the chief of police in the small town of Williams Peak for sixteen years. Before that he patrolled the streets. Born and raised there, Russ was three years from retiring and nothing surprised him anymore. Certainly not an accident on the highway at the notorious Broke Man's Curve. What did surprise him about the four in the morning phone call was after hearing about the wreckage not only was the victim alive, but he was also relatively fine.

That was the information Russ was given.

He'd see for himself when he went to the site. But first he wanted to stop by the hospital.

Williams Peak had a good little rural hospital. It was rated in the top twenty. Forty beds, an ER, a four bed ICU. It had it all, and a lot of folks from close small towns came there instead of the bigger cities.

Russ had brewed some coffee and put it in that obnoxious looking travel mug his daughter had gotten him for Christmas. It looked horrendous with a cheese curl design, but it kept a large amount of coffee piping hot for a while.

He left the mug in his car when he went inside the Emergency Room to enquire about the John Doe.

As soon as Russ stepped inside the hospital Old Joe Baker jumped from the waiting room chair and rushed to him.

Not that Joe was old, maybe some would consider him that, he was about the same age as Russ. He got the name 'old Joe' because he constantly talked about the way things had been.

A humble man who fixed cars in a garage he built on his own property. He and his wife Margorie owned the local market and café. And despite the ups and downs and the hard times, Baker's Market was still going. Just like the town.

"Hey, Chief," Joe approached him. "I can tell—"

"Not right now, Joe." Russ held up his hand, speaking politely. "I'll be with you in a minute. I'm here on business."

"I know."

"Good." With a nod Russ walked away.

"You'll be wanting to talk to me.'

"I'm sure." Russ glanced at the reception nurse who gave him a 'go ahead' to continue into the back. The second he stepped through the thick double doors he could hear the yelling. It came from the back. A male voice, kind of raspy, but with that loud, angry, gurgling sound.

"Let me go! Now! Now!" Pause. "I don't care! Let … me … go!"

Russ shifted his eyes about, wondering how he didn't hear that yelling when he walked in.

What was going on?

Doc Jenner was behind the nurse's station. When he first came to the hospital, he was young and wet behind the ears. He had just finished his residency in some Chicago hospital. He thought he knew it all, but he didn't know people.

It was like some old movie watching the change in the doc.

That was twenty some years earlier.

"Russ," Doc said with an exhausted voice. "Glad you finally got here."

Russ readied to reply but instead lifted his head to the yelling.

"No! I don't care. No." the man shouted.

"Is he yelling at himself?" Russ asked.

"Just reacting to Janey, but you know her, it doesn't faze her," Doc replied.

"You need him arrested?"

"Sedated. But I figured you might want to ask him questions first."

"The patient yelling is our accident victim?" Russ asked.

"Our only patient right now, yes."

"How long has he been like that?"

"Not long. He's combative. You'll see. At least he's speaking words now."

"What do you mean?"

"He wasn't making any words when he first came to. He was out cold when he arrived. This way." Doc Jenner led the way down to the treatment area.

It was a small emergency room. Only six rooms and they had him in the last one.

Russ stopped the doctor before they went into the treatment room. "How is he physically, Doc?"

"Well, he's gonna be all kinds of shades of blue and purple, but surprisingly, other than a couple sutures to the face, nothing is broken. No fractures. No internal bleeding."

"So, we don't need to transfer him to another hospital?"

"Nope, we can handle his injuries." Jenner winced when the man yelled again. "This ... needs sedation." He slid open the glass door to the treatment room, then the curtain.

The nurse Janey was behind a computer. "Oh," she said with a smile. "Good. I'll go get the sedative ready. All yours." She pushed the rolling stand with the computer past Doc Jenner and Russ.

Russ stepped in. The young man in bed wasn't what he expected. He expected someone bigger by the voice. He was not bigger than maybe five-nine, average built, his brown hair was a matted mess and his face had tiny scratches all over it.

The young man growled, trying to lift up but was restrained.

"You called the cops?" his voice squeaked. "You called the cops! Good! Good." He looked at Russ. "You think you scare me? Huh? You don't scare me."

"I don't expect I do scare you," Russ said calmly. "What's your name, son?"

The young man went silent, even stopped fighting the restraints.

"He's not saying or he doesn't know," Doc Jenner said.

"Let me out of here! I'll go with you, I swear."

"Go where?" Russ asked.

"To find him."

"Find who?"

"The man. There was a man in the car with me!" he screamed. "He's gone."

"You mean he died in the accident?" Russ asked.

"No, he's gone!" The young man growled out with a scream.

"So, someone was with you?"

"Yes! I've been trying to tell them!"

"Can you tell me your name, son?" Russ asked again.

The young man twisted and turned and growled again.

Doc Jenner waved his finger at the young man. "I told you, keep doing that and you'll feel it in the morning."

Russ sighed out. "I don't think I'm getting anything out of him tonight. Was there anything in his pockets? Any ID?"

Doc Jenner shook his head. "Nothing."

"I'm heading up to the site now. State police are there. They may have found out who he is. We'll check the plates."

"Is Donnie up there?" Doc asked.

"I'm gonna guess he is, he works nights, and you know your son is always Johnny on the spot when there's an accident, especially Broke Man's Curve. Say ..." he lowered his voice. "Do you think there was someone else in the car?"

"I couldn't tell you."

"We'll look."

"I'm here!" the man screamed. "I'm right here!"

Russ looked at him. "Well, I'm glad you told me that. Thank you." He returned to Jenner. "Do me a favor. Get me a BAL."

"We did."

"And?"

Doc Jenner shook his head. "Barely traceable amount, like cough syrup level."

"Do a drug panel."

"We did that, too," Doc Jenner replied. "Nothing. But ... it was a fast track and urine, when Dale gets to the lab in the morning, he'll run the blood we took. Get a better idea. But it's not alcohol, I can say that with all assurance."

Russ looked back at the patient then stepped out of the room with Doc Jenner. "He's got to be on something."

"You would think."

"Head injury?" Russ asked.

"That's our guess. We'll know more when we get the blood work back. But now, no fracture of the skull, no brain bleeding. Accident like that, I'm sure he hit his head. We'll do another scan in the morning," Doc Jenner said. "Old Joe said he was thrown, but I didn't see any signs of that."

"Old Joe?" Russ questioned. "How would Old Joe know?"

"He's the one that found him."

Russ whined a little with a slight stomp of his foot. He knew what that meant. He had to talk to Old Joe. Nothing was wrong with him, Russ liked him and all, but Old Joe was long winded, and Russ just wanted to get to the scene of the accident.

"Told you," Old Joe said, smugly when Russ approached him.

"Yes, you did. Now, you can tell me how you happened upon that boy in the middle of the night."

"Well, Marge and I were at that new casino across the state line," Joe said. "You know the one they built ..."

"Yeah, yeah, go on."

"Marge just loves that casino. Not that we won anything, but it was tough to get her off this one machine."

"Joe, just tell me what happened." Russ tried to keep his patience.

"We were coming back on Eighty West, and as we approached Broke Man's curve, we saw a deer in the road. We slowed, always do on that curve, and sure enough, when we were halfway through that curve, there was that boy in the middle of the road praying."

"Wait ... he was what?"

"Praying."

"And you know this how?"

"He was there, middle of the road, on his knees, looking up."

"Okay."

"He was praying," Joe said. "Because he saw us barreling his way, he didn't have that deer in the headlights look, he wasn't afraid."

"That's because he's on something."

Joe shook his head. "No. That's because he was confident, he wasn't going to die because Jesus was in the car with him."

"Metaphorically like the song?" Russ asked.

"Nope. In the car," Joe said. "He told us someone was in the car with him. A man."

"And you assumed it was Jesus?" Russ asked.

"Yep. You don't survive a crash like that if He isn't in that car with you."

With a thinking, 'hmm', Russ nodded. "You gotta point. But ... I have to work on the assumption that maybe someone else was in that car with him. I'm headed up to the site, thanks for your help." He took a few steps away and stopped. "However, just in case, once it gets to a decent hour, give Pastor Rick a call. See if he'll pay a visit to our John Doe, maybe he'll talk to the pastor."

"Will do, Chief."

Russ thanked him again and headed out.

Russ could see the flashing lights of the state police long before he arrived at the accident site.

The flatbed tow truck was the first vehicle he had seen, then the fire truck. The firefighters were rolling the hoses, while a state police officer directed what little traffic there was around the accident. There was an ambulance there, the lights weren't on. And Russ could still see the lingering smoke as it floated through the rays of the spotlights.

He saw State Trooper Donnie Jenner, the doctor's son, standing outside his squad car.

"Hey, Donnie," Russ extended his hand to him. "Glad to see you up here."

"Chief." Donnie shook his hand. "You didn't need to come out. I could have brought you the report."

"I was getting up anyway. How did it happen? Any ideas? Old Joe mentioned a deer."

Donnie nodded. "That's what we're going with, coming around Broke Man's curve, deer was there, he didn't react fast enough. It was a pretty violent crash, Chief. I can't believe he walked away from it."

"Yeah. You aren't kidding. Any ... uh, identification on the vehicle."

"Frame is still hot," Donnie replied. "We didn't see anything in the glove box. Plate was burned beyond recognition."

"How about the vin?"

"We are going to try to salvage it. We're hopeful."

Russ nodded. "The kid said there was someone in the car with him."

"That's what we heard. We've been searching."

"Could he have been thrown?" Russ asked. "Back at the curve and he's not been spotted? You're too young to remember, but in seventy-six, three weeks after that accident they found the body of the other passenger."

"True, but ..." Donnie said, "In 1976 no one survived to say there were two people in that car. We know. We're looking. Once it's light, we'll be able to see what we can find."

"Good boy." Russ gave a swat to Donnie's arm. "I knew you guys would be ..." his words slowed down when he finally saw her standing on the side of the road. "Excuse me for a second."

Shaking his head in a bit of disbelief, Russ walked over to Marjorie Baker.

She stood on the berm looking down the embankment. Her

arms were folded tight to her body, as if she fought off a chill.

Everyone, including Russ, really liked Marge. She was just a good woman with a big heart. Marge was younger than Old Joe by a good ten years. But Russ always said she was one of the wisest, kindest people he had met. Just looking at her was a welcoming sight. A fuller built woman with auburn-brown hair styled in a way she hadn't changed in decades. Her smile was genuine and gentle. She was the person everyone wanted around when things went bad. Always the one to give them 'mama style' hugs that took it all away.

It was no surprise she was there.

Marge was so focused staring out she didn't see Russ approach.

"Morning, Marge."

"Oh." She jumped a little, her hand shooting to her chest. "You scared me."

"What are you doing out here at four in the morning?"

Her eyes went forward again. "Praying. You know. Making sure our workers are safe and ..." she sighed heavily. "Praying for the other person in the car. That they find him."

"You know your husband is convinced it was Jesus in the car."

"Oh, no doubt Jesus was in that car in one capacity or another. Look at it. Look at that car, Russ. It's destroyed. No one should have walked away from that, and I fear if there was another physical human being in the car, he wasn't as fortunate as that young man." She glanced at Russ. "I keep thinking about the infamous crash of seventy-six."

"Me, too. Marge ... was it you who called it in?" Russ asked.

"Yes. I called. Joe took him into the hospital. It was closer and faster than calling for an ambulance. Plus, we knew, or at least it looked like he didn't have any life threatening injuries."

"I know this is a tough one to ask you," Russ said. "Do you think he was on something? Joe said he looked like he had no fear of getting hit by your car."

"On something I don't know. All I saw was someone so lost."

"And he was conscious when he got in the car?"

Marge nodded. "When we put him in, yes. He kept saying someone was with him. Someone was in his car."

"Anything else?"

"He said 'Thank you.'"

"Huh. He wasn't angry? Out of control?"

Marge bit down on her bottom lip as she shook her head. "Why?"

"Well, he's being pretty brazen now, combative. By any chance, did he give you his name?"

"I don't think he knows his name. He didn't know much. Trust me. This accident was traumatic. It took the wind out of him physically and mentally."

"We'll figure out it," Russ said with confidence.

"I know you will. I have a feeling, just a feeling, that young man is gonna need more help," Marge said. "Than just figuring out his name."

SEVEN

"I got you."

Jonas didn't know the voice, but it was a part of his dream as he woke up. The room was sunny and bright, a slight cast of yellow peeked through the window, letting him know it was morning. It felt like it.

But that was all he knew.

The events of the night before were a blur, in fact everything was a blur. Where was he? How did he get there? Who … was he?

It was like trying to remember a name, one of those 'tip of the tongue' feelings, but it wasn't simply about a name. It was about his life.

He turned his head from the window to look at the other side of the room, never even knowing a nurse was there fixing a tube that ran into his arm.

She gave a closed mouth smile and finished her work. "Would you like some water?" she asked.

Jonas nodded. His mouth and lips were dry. In fact, his lips felt huge and his eyes sore, like he had been crying.

He accepted the water taking a few long drinks. "Thank you," he said. "My face feels funny."

"You have a lot of bruising, some stitches. Heard they pulled quite a bit of glass out of your face in the ER." She stepped back and rolled the tray cart to him. "They brought your breakfast. Are you hungry? Looks like …" she lifted the lid. "Coffee, eggs, bacon, toast and I think … this is oatmeal."

Jonas tried to absorb how he physically felt, he knew his head hurt, but was he hungry? He tried to sit up and when he moved, every part of his body hurt. When his arms felt heavy, he was concerned until he looked down and saw he was bound with canvas straps.

"What … why? Why am I tied to the bed?"

"Last night you were pretty bad," she said. "I wasn't on shift, but the notes say you were violent and thrashing. They sedated you. If you're hungry, I'll be happy to feed you."

"Yeah, that would be good. Thanks. I think … I think I'm fine now though."

"I'll talk to the doctor about those restraints," she said, unwrapping the eating utensils.

"Maybe it isn't a good idea to untie me."

"Why do you say that?" she asked with a smile.

"What if I was violent because I'm a like a killer or something?"

"That's a strange thing to say. Why?"

"I feel angry. I don't know why. It just feels like anger."

"I don't know why that is. Maybe something happened before the accident. Hopefully, you're not a killer." She handed him the strip of bacon to take a bite.

"The accident." Jonas took a bite. "I don't remember it. There was a man with me. I remember him. He was in the car."

"That's what everyone heard." She gave him some eggs. "They have been searching for him. All night I think."

"Anything?"

She shook her head. "No, everyone is just hoping it's not another nineteen-seventy-six."

"What is that?"

"Around here it's a legend," she replied. "You crashed on Broke Man's Curve. Famous for crashes. It was named this because in the fifties a man who was destitute crashed his car there on purpose."

"But what happened in seventy-six?"

"Nothing you should really worry about. A missing passenger thing,"

"Like me?"

"Not like you. You survived."

"Why don't I know who I am?" he asked.

"You have a head injury, and the doctor will be in shortly to talk to you. I promise."

She finished feeding him, Jonas didn't really want much. He told her he had enough when his stomach started to feel queasy.

He rested his head back and closed his eyes. He was tired again. Sleeping was better than being awake, with a feeling of frustration and confusion he closed his eyes.

He had fallen asleep. Jonas was sure of it, he didn't know for how long. The man's voice asking, "Are you awake in there?" Caused him to open his eyes.

"Good. Good." The man was wearing a white coat over his hospital scrubs. He lifted a light to Jonas' eyes. "Just want to check those pupils." He did his thing then put the light away. "How are you feeling?"

"Very sore."

"You'll have that. I'm Doctor Jenner. And you are our celebrity patient."

"I'm famous?" Jonas asked.

"Well, not in the Kardashian sense, no." he shook his head. "A stranger gets into an accident on Broke Man's curve and lives to talk about it. That earns them celebrity status. Then again, how that is, honestly, we still can't figure out."

"I can't remember it. I feel awake though. I remember the nurse feeding me. I think."

"And that's your first memory? Ann feeding you?"

"First clear one, yeah," he nodded.

"You don't remember last night?"

"No. Well, it's foggy, but not really."

"You have a head injury. We did another scan late last night," Doctor Jenner said. "I wasn't satisfied with the first one. With your behavior and all. Definitely showed some swelling. Because of that, we are going to have you stay in here a few days. Once that swelling goes down, I'm confident you'll regain your memory. Or shortly after."

"What if I don't?"

Doctor Jenner shook his head. "We can't think like that."

"I mean, how do I know how to talk, but not who I am?"

"Head injuries are a mysterious territory. We don't know how the brain works. So …" Jenner exhaled. "Ann, the nurse, tells me you don't want the restraints removed because you're worried that you're a serial killer."

"I don't know who I am. I do feel really angry right now. I don't know why, and I feel like anything can set me off."

"How about once we find out you're not a killer, we remove those restraints. Some mood stabilizers might help. Head injuries can cause severe mood swings."

"Whatever you think."

"Good. And don't you worry about your memory," Jenner said. "It'll come back. Either in bits and pieces or something will set it off and bam, you'll remember. But I'm confident you'll remember."

Jonas studied the doctor's face, he glanced up quickly when he saw someone else enter the room. It was a police officer; an older man, and he was big.

"Am I interrupting?" the officer asked.

Doctor Jenner looked back. "No, Chief, we're just talking. Come on in."

"I was seeing how our patient was doing," the chief said. "Blood work come back yet?"

"Not yet. Dale's working on it. He's doing well. We have a concussion we're worried about," Doctor Jenner said. "Keeping him here for a few days because of it."

"Any memory?" the chief asked.

Jonas shook his head. "No, but I do remember the man. I remember the man in the car. I can see him. Did you find him?"

"Sorry, son," the chief shook his head. "We did not. We're still looking though. If he was in the car with you, we'll find him."

"If? If? He was," Jonas huffed, then noticed the badge. "What is WPPD?'

"Williams Peak Police Department," the chief answered.

"You're in Williams Peak."

"I don't know if I ever heard of it," Jonas said.

"We're a small town in Nebraska," answered the chief.

"Nebraska!" Jonas spat with shock. "Why do I feel like I'm not from Nebraska."

A new voice entered the room and conversation, a man. "Because you're not," he said, walking in.

It was another police officer, this one younger.

"Sorry," the officer said. "I couldn't resist. I heard him say that. Hey, Dad." He walked over to the doctor and kissed him on the cheek.

"Dad?" Jonas questioned.

"Donnie," the doctor said. "Have you been up all night?"

"I have," he spoke through his exhale of words. "We were able to match the VIN on the burnt car. And we think …" Donnie, the officer looked at Jonas. "We know who you are." He handed a folder to the chief. "Harold Whitmore. Twenty-nine from Kansas City, Kansas. If you look Chief, five foot nine, brown hair, brown eyes. Look at the driver's license picture."

The chief opened the folder. "Hard to say, this license is expired, and the picture has to be six years old."

"Look at the picture," Donnie said. "Take away the bruising, swelling and cuts … it's him."

The chief lifted his eye above the folder and looked at Jonas. "I suppose you're right. It is the car. Any trace of a contact, family?"

Donnie nodded. "He has one relative. A grandmother. She's in Europe now. She said as long as he was fine, she wasn't coming back for two weeks. She hasn't really talked to him in months. Harold …" Donnie dropped his voice. "Likes to do his own thing and she said he's not a nice person."

"Surprise, Surprise." The Chief grumbled and handed the folder back to Donnie. "Thank you. And get some rest."

The doctor looked at Donnie. "Did you run him? Is Harold a killer?"

"If he is, he hasn't been caught," Donnie replied. "Not even a ticket."

"How about that." Doctor Jenner placed his hand on Jonas. "You're not a killer. We can undo those restraints."

"And," the chief added. "I don't have to run your prints. Welcome to Williams Peak, Harold. At least that's one mystery solved."

Jonas sunk back into his pillow. He didn't feel any better, any less angry. If the mystery was solved, it couldn't be proved by Jonas. Maybe it was the head injury or temporary amnesia, but Harold Whitmore from Kansas just didn't feel right.

EIGHT

Grant ran.

It wasn't his usual routine on a Sunday morning. Running was an evening thing for him. Typically, he basked in sleeping in late on Sundays. Then getting up and having his coffee, reading the news until Cate came back from church. Grant didn't do the church thing, never had. It wasn't his thing. Cate always said she'd get him to one day change his mind. She hadn't done it in thirty-five years, he didn't think she would. But their routine never changed. Then they'd go to lunch or shopping. It was a just a laid back day of the week for Grant.

Not on this Sunday.

He was up earlier than he thought, he tossed and turned all night.

After getting dressed and a few swigs of coffee, Grant needed to go for a run. Maybe get a jog in before Cate even woke. She'd be surprised to see him.

The weather was nice. A slight hint of fog had set in, not many people were out. He drove to the park and hit the track. Trying to clear his mind, focus on what he'd do for the day, where they'd do lunch. Avoid admitting that he thought about Jonas.

He swore the last time Jonas had a setback it was the last time he would invest his energy and emotions into worrying. He had spoken to another faculty member at the school and they gave him advice in regard to something called the three C's.

Cause. Cure. Control.

He didn't *cause* Jonas' problems.

He alone couldn't *cure* Jonas' problem and he certainly

couldn't *control* them.

Wave after wave, up and down, good and bad, it was enough to drive Grant mad. He didn't want to care. He wanted to be able to distance himself from it all. He watched what his wife went through, what she did to herself.

It was insane.

Grant went through it all, too. He just was silent about it.

When he woke, admittedly he wanted to pick up his phone or Cate's to see if Jonas replied to the text. He looked for a missed phone call, one from a number he didn't know in the middle of the night.

There was none.

That was a good thing.

No news was always good news and he kept telling himself that.

After his run, he went back home, started a pot of coffee and jumped in the shower.

Cate was surprised he was up. Not surprised he wasn't joining her.

He saw that look on Cate's face when she checked her phone.

What she showed facially, he felt inside.

"His phone probably died," Grant told her. "Go to church, when you get back, we'll call. It'll be check out time at whatever hotel they stayed at."

Cate agreed, reluctantly. Although Grant wasn't sure she wouldn't try to call Jonas on the way to services.

But Grant was nowhere near as calm and reasonable as he projected. Against what he wanted to do, the moment Cate left, he called their daughter.

"I know you don't like when we do this to you," he said to her. "Have you spoken to your brother?"

He heard her make that sigh. The 'really, are we doing this again?' sound she so often made.

"No," she replied. "I mean, He sent a text yesterday he had a gig and was headed to your house."

"But not after that?" he asked.

"No. Is everything okay?"

"I don't know. He hasn't replied to your mom's texts and when I called it goes straight to voicemail."

"His phone probably died. I know the gig wasn't close."

"That's what has me worried. And him and I got into it before he left."

"Why?"

"He was drinking and I wouldn't give him my truck."

"I don't blame you," she said. "I think he's fine. Okay? Just being a jerk and making you guys worry. He probably rode with Brett."

"Who's Brett?" Grant asked.

"The drummer. Have you checked his social media?" Jessie asked.

"We're not friends with him. I guess it's not cool to be friends with your parents on social media."

"Hold on."

Grant could hear his daughter talking to her husband, asking him to check on social media for Jonas. "Okay, he hasn't posted for a couple days. Tell you what, I'll message Brett. I'll have him reach out to you. Okay? I'm sure my brother is fine."

"I am, too. But ... you know, your mom has me worried. And on a different note, are you guys coming for dinner? I promise no Jonas talk."

Jessie chuckled. "We'll be there."

Grant thanked his daughter, feeling bad he even had to call her. It seemed that Jonas' behavior always dragged her into the drama and it wasn't fair.

She was the epitome of 'you are your brother's keeper' always the one who talked to him when things were bad. Always overshadowed by her brother's bad behavior.

Grant felt stupid.

What was he doing?

Jonas was a grown man. Thirty-two years old. Mistakes were for him to make, not for Grant to try to cut off or fix.

The bottom line was Jonas was his child. No matter how old,

he was still his child.

Cate returned from church and as usual after services, she had an optimistic attitude. Her worrisome attitude from the night before seemed to be buried.

Unlike Grant, she seemed less worried about not hearing from Jonas and more irritated that he would do this.

Their Sunday lunch spot was Sandy's Diner. A small spot Grant had found when they first moved to town years earlier. It was a place they took the kids. Like Grant, they always got breakfast, no matter what time of day it was. Cate preferred a sandwich.

Now they were alone, empty nesters they were called.

Cate enjoyed the lunches with her husband. He was a good man, looked almost as young as the day she met him. Sure, his face had a few lines, but he was still handsome. The gray in his hair was masked by his natural, sandy, blonde hair. Granted he put off getting a haircut as long as possible. As they sat in the diner, it was at that phase where the bangs curled up, some dancing across the tops of his wire rim glasses.

To Cate, he was a little less talkative than usual. He was preoccupied and doing that thing where he tried too hard to hide the fact something was bothering him.

She didn't want to prod, eventually he'd open up about it. He never really was good at keeping things inside.

Midway through the lunch, his message alert sounded off. In an unusual occurrence, Grant looked at his phone. He lifted his eyes to Cate.

"What is it?" she asked.

"I need to make a phone call."

"Sure."

The phone was in his hand, and after a swipe of his thumb on the screen, he brought it to his ear. "Hey, yeah, thank you so much for reaching out." He paused. "I know it's weird. And I'm really sorry, but we haven't heard from Jonas and ..." His facial expression suddenly switched to concern as he listened. "At all? Who did he drive with?" Grant's eyes closed. "Yes, please. Call me right back. Thank you." Slowly, he set down the phone.

"What?" Cate could feel that panic, the feeling she had left behind when she walked into church. "What is it?"

Grant hesitated before answering. "That was Jonas' drummer, Brett. No one has seen or heard from Jonas since they left the club. He was still there. He never made it back to the hotel. Brett is actually a block away from Jonas' place now. He's checking there."

"And he'll get right back to us?" Cate asked, shivering an exhaling breath.

"Yes, he said he'll get right back. Maybe ... maybe he met someone." Grant shrugged. "He said he was still at the club. He met some people. Did his partying thing and is sleeping it off. That wouldn't be out of character for him."

"No, it wouldn't be." Cate lifted her coffee.

"We won't worry until we have to," Grant said. "Right."

"Right."

Grant's eyes kept shifting to the phone. He mentioned not worrying, but said nothing about relaxing. She knew neither one of them would relax until after his phone rang again.

NINE

"I got you."

It was him. The man in the car, David. The vision of him flashed before Jonas' eyes. It happened out of the blue while he aimed the remote at the television. There wasn't anything that triggered it, at least none he knew. But it came to him.

It was dark, it was after the accident. Jonas was reaching, his hands bloody and David suddenly appeared, his face drew close to Jonas. "I got you."

Gone.

That was it.

But it was a start. It was his first memory of the accident, if indeed it was a memory.

"Hi, there, Harold!"

Who was the old guy that just poked his head in the door of his hospital room?

Jonas just stared.

"Want some visitors?"

What Jonas wanted to say was, "Do I have a choice?' but he refrained and said nothing.

Had he known the old guy wasn't alone, he may have said something.

A man walked in with him, a little younger than the older guy and with them also was a woman. Younger, maybe Jonas' age or around that, she held an iPad or something in her hands.

The guys stepped closer. "You look ... well, I'd say good, but you look kind of swollen in the face. Anyhow, visitors in the hospital are good for the soul and healing. Since you don't have any family in town, Pastor Rick here thought it'd might be nice to send some visitors your way to keep up the spirits."

"I don't need a priest," Jonas said.

"I'm not a priest," Pastor Rick said. "I'm a pastor and this is my daughter, Haley."

"Hi," she said politely.

"And who is he?" Jonas pointed to the old guy.

"You don't remember me?" he asked. "I'm Joe. Joe Baker. My wife and I were the ones that found you on the road. I brought you to the ER."

"Oh." Jonas nodded.

"Oh?" Haley questioned. "Just oh."

"Haley," Pastor Rick said with some reprimand.

"No, Dad, he should be saying, 'Oh, thank you'. Because it could have been someone else barreling around Broke Man's Curve. Someone that wouldn't have seen him."

"Thanks," Jonas said.

"Sure. Sure thing," Joe replied. "The staff has been telling us you haven't been in a good mood."

"Um, no," Jonas snapped. "I'm in a hospital, my body hurts, my head is splitting, and I haven't a clue who I am or what is going on."

"Then even better I brought the pastor," Joe said. "Thought you'd want him to pray with you being it is Sunday, and you didn't go to church."

"Why ... why would you think that?" Jonas asked.

"Because when I found you, you were praying in the middle of the road."

"I highly doubt that. I don't feel like I pray. I would think I would know if that was my thing," Jonas replied.

"It is your thing," Haley chimed in. "According to your social media, you go to church every Sunday." She looked up from her tablet. "You've lost a lot of weight since these pictures. Then again, the most recent one of you was three years ago."

"Look," Jonas hissed. "I didn't ask for visitors. All day long someone has been in here. The police this morning, some lady with books ..."

"That would be Louise the volunteer," Joe said. "She goes in everyone's room."

"Whatever. Just … go. Thanks. I'm fine."

Pastor Rick nodded. "We'll go. Come on, Joe, he's not feeling up to it." He stepped back. "I'll pray for you, son."

"You don't need to do that."

"No. No I don't," Pastor Rick replied. "But I will." He glanced at his daughter. "Haley?"

"I'll be right there, Dad."

Jonas watched Pastor Rick and Joe leave, then looked over at Haley who leaned against the window ledge staring down to the tablet.

"What?" he asked her. "Why did you stay?"

"Oh, I thought maybe you wanted to know about your life, Harold. You have some stuff, not much, on your social media."

"No. And why does everyone keep calling me Harold?'

"That's your name."

"No, it's not."

"Do you prefer Harry?"

"No! I'm not Harold."

"If you don't remember who you are, then how do you know your name's not Harold?"

"I just do."

"Do you remember having a thing for cute kitten posts?" She showed him the tablet.

"That's not me. I wouldn't do that."

"Again, how do you know if you don't remember?"

"Just … go. Okay. Leave. Not to be rude—"

"But you are," Haley cut him off. "You're rude. You can be sick, grumpy, even mad …" she lowered the tablet and walked closer to the bed. "But rudeness is inexcusable. Especially when there are good people trying to be nice to you."

"I suppose like you."

She laughed. "No, not like me. I'm a nice person, but I'll tell you like it is. Some won't. Like Old Joe. He'll never say a mean word, and if he comes in here again, he is the last person that deserves your rudeness. He saved you on that road."

"He shouldn't have. He should have just let me die."

"What?" Haley asked.

"Because is this my life now? Why do I want to live without even knowing if I actually have anything to live for? Without knowing who I am."

"Maybe there's a reason for it," she said.

Jonas scoffed. "A reason for what? My not knowing? Me not remembering?"

"Yep." She nodded. "Maybe for a spell, you're not supposed to." She walked around, pausing at the end of his bed before leaving. "Have a good day, Harold Whitmore."

"I'm not ..." Jonas grunted as she left. "Harold Whitmore!" After blasting that, he slammed his fist into the bed and groaned. "At least I don't think I am."

The Chief was on the phone, rocking back and forth in his chair behind his desk. He gave a signal to Pastor Rick to 'have a seat', conveying through hand movement and facial expressions that he'd be with him in a moment.

The pastor took a seat across from him.

"Yes, ma'am I understand," Russ said. "Yes, Ma'am, we appreciate it. Thank you again. Absolutely. Thank you." He set down the phone. "Wow."

"You were awfully polite," the pastor said.

"I usually am."

"That's true."

"What can I do for you, Pastor? Isn't this like your big day?"

Pastor Rick smiled. "You can say that. Anyhow, you know how we came up with that plan. Help a new stranger in need? Surround him with love and light, keep him company."

"Are you talking about Harold?"

"I am. I spoke about him in service this morning. Everyone is very impressed he survived. He's looked at like a miracle."

"Is Old Joe telling your congregation Harold was with Jesus?"

Pastor Rick shook his head. "Chief, you don't even need to tell people Jesus was there. All they hear is a young man survived a non-survivable car crash all while saying a stranger was in the car with him and he disappeared. They draw their own conclusions."

"Has Harold drawn that conclusion?"

Pastor Rick chuckled. "In my brief meeting with him, I find it hard to believe he believes in anything."

"Is he still testy?"

"That's an understatement. I want to bring in the big guns to settle him ..."

"Big guns, meaning Marge?" Russ asked.

"Yep, but she left for the sweet corn junket. She would smooth him over."

"You would think someone who walked away pretty much from an accident unscathed, one that should have killed them would instantly have a different outlook."

"You would think," Pastor Rick said. "But it might take more or longer. Who are we to say the accident didn't make him angry?"

"We are not to say," Russ replied. "But his grandmother is. I just spoke to her." He nodded at the phone. "I finally got through. She said our Harold is not a very nice person. However, she is coming to claim him. She'll be here the day after tomorrow, that is the soonest she can leave Paris."

"So, the amnesia isn't helping his persona?" the Pastor asked.

"Doesn't look that way. But I think you can call off the goodwill efforts. I understand it was started because he was alone, didn't know who he was ..."

"He still doesn't."

"We do," Russ said. "And that's good enough. His grandmother can take him and find him the doctors he needs. We don't need to waste our time trying to be nice to a bad seed."

"Ah, now see, Chief. I don't believe anyone is a bad seed.

Everyone has good in them. You just have to find it. God makes it a little difficult, but He always has a plan."

"Well, your plan may be to guide him ..."

"It is."

"My plan is to get that boy out of town, but not before citing him for a bunch of things."

"Are you serious?" Pastor Rick asked.

"The law is the law, Pastor. He broke that law when he got behind the wheel of that car under the influence. It wasn't any freak accident."

"So, he had a high blood alcohol level?"

Russ shook his head. "No, but it was something else. His behavior, I'm all too familiar with that reaction. He was on something; we're just waiting for the blood test to ..." He glanced behind him and Doc Jenner stood in the doorway. "Speak of the devil. Sorry Pastor."

Pastor Rick just shook his head.

Doc Jenner walked in. "I have been calling and texting you," he said.

"Sorry," Russ replied. "I have been on the phone for an hour. What's up?

Pastor Rick asked. "Did you need me to leave?"

"Nah, that's okay. We don't really worry about HIPPA laws." He set a folder on the chief's desk. "Dale ran the bloodwork on our Harold Whitmore."

"And?" Russ asked.

"The only thing we found was GHB."

Pastor Rick shook his head confused. "I'm sorry, what is GHB?"

Doc Jenner replied, "Gamma Hydroxybutyrate."

Russ added, "It is found in ecstasy. It's called a club drug."

"Or," Doc Jenner said. "A date rape drug."

Pastor Rick stammered some. "I ... I ... I don't understand. Why would someone deliberately take a date rape drug?"

"He took ecstasy," Russ said. "That's what it was."

"Nope." Doc Jenner shook his head. "The levels were not

consistent with ecstasy. See, the levels of GHB drop fast, they disappear, usually within eight hours even in the blood tests. Dale said he was given the GHB not long before the accident. So, either someone wanted to have their way with our accident man or ..."

Pastor Rick sunk into his chair with a heavy sigh. "They wanted him to die. They knew full well he was getting in the car." He glanced at the chief. "Still want to cite him Russ?"

"I don't know." Russ shrugged. "If someone wanted to kill that boy it confirms he is a lot of trouble. A lot more than we see. You still want to follow God's plan and guide him?"

"Actually, yes," Pastor Rick replied. "Now, more than ever."

"I hear you Pastor, I do," Russ said. "Just like I have to ask my self is it worthy of my time to cite him, you have to ask yourself is he worthy enough of your time to help."

"That's where we differ, Chief. In my opinion," Pastor Rick said. "Everyone is worthy."

TEN

Cate watched her husband. He was literally beside himself and that was strange for him. At least him showing it.

He paced as he spoke on the phone, out of earshot then back in. It was hard for her to piece together what was being said. She knew it was the police calling back and when the conversation stretched into several minutes, she relaxed knowing it wasn't bad news.

She worried it was.

They had stopped by the local police station earlier and they said they'd get back to them.

That didn't set well with Grant. She supposed, like her, he felt helpless.

He had gone on his own to Jonas' apartment and to talk to his band mates. Grant even cancelled dinner with Jessie because he said he couldn't keep his promise not to talk about Jonas.

That wasn't fair to Jessie. She always got pushed aside when Jonas caused concern.

After that, he sat at the piano biding time and tinkling random keys until the police called him back.

Finally, Cate heard the conversation end. Grant returned to the kitchen, nearly slamming his cell phone on the counter. He released it with such emotion it spun.

"What did they say?" Cate asked.

He shook his head and turned around. "They said they'll make it an official missing person's report in three days."

"Did they say why the wait?"

"I don't know, Cate," Grant hissed in frustration. "Maybe because he's an addict, maybe because they talked to the bartender and she said he left the bar alone. Maybe because he's done this before. Who knows why? I told them Brett said he was fine. Angry about the fight, but fine."

"Did they say when they talked to the bartender if she saw him drive off?"

"She told the police when she left there were no cars in the parking lot.

"You think he's just sleeping like you said earlier?"

"I don't know." Grant shook his head. "The police said they called the Iowa State police, there were no accidents. He's not been arrested. That we know of."

"But they checked?"

Grant nodded. "That's what he said."

"Do you think he's sleeping it off somewhere like you said earlier?"

"I don't know, Cate, it's eight o'clock at night. Although, he's ... done it before."

"Do you think ...?"

"Cate!" he cut her off.

"Grant, please don't get angry with me, I'm upset, too."

"Then show it. Show it. Oh, wait, that's right, the sun is still up."

Cate scoffed a laugh. "What is that supposed to mean?"

"It means your neuroticism has a schedule. Weekends are the worst and, like last night, you're ready to jump out of your skin thinking 'that' phone call is going to come. But, hey, when the sun comes up, you go to church and everything is fine."

"That's not it, Grant." Cate stood. "It's because when the sun comes up, I realized how foolish I was getting over things I can't control. And I'm calm after church because I feel at peace afterwards. That's not to say in a few more hours I won't be jumping out of my skin again."

"I'm sorry." He exhaled and embraced her. "I don't know why I am so uptight about this. You know, it's not like it's unusual for him to go missing for a couple of days."

"Maybe because you guys were arguing?" Cate asked.

"That's probably it. You know ..." He cleared his throat and stepped back. "When you and I talked about the tough love thing, you used to say you didn't want to do tough love and distance yourself then carry the guilt if something happened. I didn't get it. I do now. I have been doing this tough love with him since his last stunt."

"Grant, you've been doing the tough love thing with Jonas his whole life."

"Are you saying his problems are my fault?" Grant asked.

"What? No. Where is that coming from?" Cate spoke emotionally. "His problems are no one's fault but his own. I'm saying you've always been firm with him. Especially the last several years."

Grant puckered his lips some, drawing in his emotions. "It's been hard. Everything he was as a boy has been overshadowed by what he has become as a man. And I stopped seeing that little boy. I miss him. I .... I don't even know the last time I told him I loved him."

"Grant ..."

"No." Grant held up his hand, shaking his head. "It's the what if. What if we never see him again? What was the last thing we said to each other? I'll tell you, we didn't part pleasantly. I ..." In his own frustration, he grunted and stopped speaking.

"When he did this two years ago ... I couldn't stop crying. Every time I closed my eyes, I'd see him in trouble. As much as I love Jonas, I can't do this to myself again."

Grant emotionally chuckled, "Are you saying you're going to be the calm one?"

"I have news for you, you're really not that calm. Just good at hiding it."

Grant gave his silent agreement with a slight lowering of his head.

"Over the years, I have asked God so many times to send his angels to watch over him and I believe He did, that's why we still have our son. I have no reason to believe He doesn't have them out there with Jonas this time."

"I wish I had your belief," Grant told her. "I wish I believed it so easily and with so much faith."

"It's not as easy as I make it look. I mean like I give it to God, then you know, snatch it right back. But He only really lets me think I took it back."

Once more, Grant stepped in and embraced Cate. "You gave it to God, I gave it to the police. Either way," he said. "It's out of our hands."

ELEVEN

Nothing made sense to him. Not the small town he viewed from his hospital window, or even the fact there was a hospital in a place that didn't look like it held a lot of people. But what did Jonas know? He was like a foreigner in a new land, only he was a foreigner in his own mind.

It had been four days since the accident. They told him it happened very early on a Sunday—he didn't know that. Here it was Wednesday, and nothing had come back to him.

Although, it was only the day before the swelling went down. Doctor Jenner said it wouldn't take long, something would make it click.

Nothing had yet.

Jonas stared at the social media account of Harold, he visited the friends' pages hoping something, anything would click.

It didn't.

None of the pictures of the trips Harold took or parties he went to.

Harold hadn't updated his page in a long time, like he was hiding, which made him wonder if he indeed was Harold.

He saw the resemblance in the face even though Harold had to be seventy-pounds heavier.

The only thing Jonas remembered was seeing the mystery passenger's face looking at him, saying. "I got you."

Did that even happen? For all Jonas knew it was his imagination, because he knew nothing else about that night. How he got into the accident or even out of the car and to the hospital.

He was having feelings though, things he couldn't make

sense of.

If he was really Harold then once the grandmother showed up, perhaps she could fill in the blanks.

She was finally coming, delay after delay, last he heard from the Chief of Police she had landed at the airport.

Doctor Jenner still did not want to release him, but he heard from a nurse it looked as if his grandmother was rich, so she would move him somewhere better.

Anywhere was better, the Williams Peak Hospital was just so ... plain and basic. Not that Jonas knew differently.

He spent a lot of time staring out that window, he probably knew every shop in the radius he could see from his room.

What else was he going to do? Look out the window, watch television, eat.

"If I am going to come here," the woman's voice entered the room. "I really prefer not seeing your fanny poking out the back of your gown."

He slowly turned from the window to see the woman standing by the doorway. She was wearing a running suit. Not one she would exercise in, one more for comfort. She didn't look rich.

"Are you the grandmother?" he asked.

"The ... grandmother? Or Harold's grandmother?" She stepped inside, set one of those paper shopping bags with the handles, along with her purse on the chair under the television. "No. I'm not."

"I thought you might be her. She's supposed to get me out."

"I heard that, too."

"I told them no visitors."

"And I don't care." She stepped to him. "You look much better than the last time I saw you."

Instantly, there was something calming about her. He didn't know the woman, but her eyes were so genuine and kind.

"We spoke before?" he asked.

"Barely. My husband and I were the ones who found you on the road," she said. "I'm Marge. Some call me Margorie, Margie, or like most ... Maw-Maw." She pulled forth the other chair.

"Mind if I sit? Doesn't matter if you do." She sat. "That feels better. Why don't you have a seat? The window seat is nice, although you might catch a draft from the air conditioning."

Jonas backed up and sat on the bed. "They call you Maw-Maw? Who calls you Maw-Maw?"

"The little ones. But some of the little ones are grown like you and their littles ones call me that."

"Well, some people call me Harold."

"That's what I heard."

"I don't believe it though. It doesn't ... feel right."

"Well, if it makes you feel better, I don't think you're Harold any more than you do."

"Why do you say that?" Jonas asked. "When everyone else does."

Marge leaned forward a little. "I saw the pictures. Harold's lifestyle is lazy. No way would he be as thin as you. Speaking of which ..." She stood and walked to the other chair, reaching in the bag. "I brought you muffins. I know you have to be hungry." Marge walked back to her chair. "I was in here once for a broken wrist. Food is bad. I know Susan who runs the food service here. She isn't that good. Don't tell anyone I said that. Anyhow, I would have been here sooner, but I was on a junket."

"What's a junket?"

"Depends on who you ask." Marge handed him a muffin. "It could be a pudding or a short trip. I had both." She smiled. "I went to the Sweet Corn Festival."

"Doesn't sound fun."

"How do you know? Last I heard you didn't remember anything."

"I don't."

"Well, a sweet corn festival might be your thing," she said. "Don't knock it." Marge inched his hand toward his mouth. "Eat your muffin."

Russ saw her before she even saw him.

It had to be her. Beatrice Whitmore. Harold's grandmother.

Not only didn't she look like she didn't belong in Williams Peak, she also didn't look like anyone from Nebraska.

He watched her step from the fancy car parked across the street. She crossed the road without looking, expecting traffic to stop for her.

Even though she was dressed to the nines, face made up, hair done, all Russ could think of was the movie Bye-Bye Birdie.

The original one. The way she walked and moved, just flashed Russ' mind to Albert's overprotective mother in the movie. Somehow, he knew this woman was not that overprotective about Harold.

Beatrice seemed annoyed, then again, Russ knew she had cut her vacation short.

"He's a very nice young man," Russ said. "We will be sad to see him …"

"Yes, yes. Where is he? Where is this hospital?"

"I'll walk you there," Russ said.

She chuckled. "No, I'll drive and meet you there."

Russ gave her the 'round about' direction so he could get there on foot before she did and warn Doctor Jenner.

But he didn't make it there fast enough to give him the entire rundown before Beatrice made her approach.

Doc tried pleasantries, but that didn't work. Beatrice was no nonsense and went straight to business. A woman more annoyed with being inconvenienced than concerned with the wellbeing of her grandson.

"Can he be moved?" she asked.

"Yes," Doctor Jenner told her. "But he should be in the hospital another few days. He sustained a head injury. And while the swelling has gone down, he doesn't remember anything. We hope when he sees you it will come back."

"I already have a neuropsychologist on call for when he gets to Lincoln. I'm having him transported there. He'll be moved tomorrow."

"We really do have the capabilities here," Jenner said.

"I'm sure. He'll be moved tomorrow. Now ... where is my grandson?"

"This way." Doctor Jenner motioned out his hand, then looked to Russ.

"What room?" she asked as she walked in the direction.

"Third room. Two-ten."

"Rold-Rold," she called out as she approached the room. "Gather your things, we will be moving you." She stepped in the room and stopped. She looked at Jonas, then spun and looked at the doctor. "Is this a joke?"

Doctor Jenner looked confused. "I don't understand."

"That ..." She pointed to Jonas. "Is not my grandson." Beatrice stormed back out of the room. "You will be hearing from my lawyers."

The Chief and Doctor Jenner stood dumbfounded as she stormed out. Doctor Jenner followed her.

Russ gave an apologetic look to Jonas. "Process of elimination. We know who you aren't. We'll figure this out." Then he, too, left the room.

Jonas plopped back on the bed. "Process of elimination." He shook his head.

Marge gave a closed mouth smile. "We will figure that out. In the meantime ... she walked back over to the paper shopping bag and reached in. "I brought you some pajamas." She handed them to him. "My son's. They might be a tad big, just pull the drawstring."

He didn't look up.

"Take them," she said.

Without looking up, he reached for them and grumbled a 'thanks'.

"You didn't think you were Harold," Marge said. "Why the

disappointment?"

"I don't know." Jonas shrugged. "I need to be somebody. Who am I?"

"Like I said, we'll figure it out. Until then ... I'm going to call you Chip."

"Chip?" Jonas asked.

"Chip."

"Why Chip?"

"Because I'm willing to bet you are a chip off somebody's block."

Jonas clenched the pajamas. "I guess I wanted to get out of here."

Marge looked at him. "You may not be well enough to be discharged, but ... I don't think there'd be any harm in going outside. Why don't you get dressed, I'll fetch a wheelchair and we'll go get some fresh air." She made her way to the door.

"I don't need you to do that for me," Jonas said. "I'm okay, you don't need to mother me."

"I don't look at it as mothering, I look at it as substituting."

"Huh?" he gazed at her confused.

"You're not Harold, but you are somebody. And I am sure you have a mother. You can look at it as me doing this for her." Marge passed a smile and walked out of the room.

Jonas was overwhelmed with a strange feeling as he sat on the bed. Maybe it was the woman Maw-Maw or even the pajamas, he didn't know. But it was the first time since he arrived at that hospital that he didn't feel angry.

TWELVE

Jessie was a blessing. She was also a badly needed diversion for Cate. Her daughter's smile could light up a room, and she was funny. She made Cate laugh about little things. The outing to the gardening store fit the bill. Even though it was crowded, Cate really didn't enjoy the store when it was packed. She supposed everyone that gardened was preparing for their annuals.

"What about these, Mom?" Jessie pointed to a pink and white flower. "They're different."

"Yes, they are but ... do I want different?"

"Why browse a gardening store if you're just going to walk out with what you always walk out with," Jessie said. "We can skip the browsing, get your stuff and head to lunch."

"You're right. Maybe I do need a change." Cate reached for the tag on the flowers to read about them.

Jessie placed her hand over Cate's. "How are you?"

"Huh?" Cate smiled.

"Stop. How are you doing?"

Cate shook her head. "That's not what today is about."

"Really? Because I'm a mess, I can only imagine how you are."

Heavily, Cate released the breath she held. "I'm sorry, sweetie. I'm sorry you're a mess."

"And you're not?"

"The first couple days were really rough. Then when the police were asking all those questions and wanted pictures, it was surreal. But to be honest with you, he's not arrested, not in the hospital anywhere. He's either out there not wanting to be found or in a ditch. Either case, as hard as it is, I can't change those circumstances."

"I keep trying his phone."

"The last ping they had from it was that bar he played," Cate said. "At least they aren't dragging the rivers yet."

"Mom, that's not funny."

"I'm not joking."

"Do we know whose car he was driving?" Jessie asked.

"He got it from Teeter."

"Teeter?" Jessie recoiled. "He's a dealer, Mom."

"I know. Bret said they're still friends."

"If he got a car from Teeter, we may not know whose car it is. People get desperate to get stuff. Have you guys talked to him?"

"We tried, he's in jail. Arrested a few days ago, but he won't talk to us."

Jessie shook her head in disgust. "He's such a piece of work. How's Dad?" Jessie asked, moving along with her mother to the next batch of flowers.

"Your father is not doing well. I know him. He's not even hiding it anymore. All the arguments and fights. The tough love. If something has happened to Jonas, your father right now is in a place where he will never forgive himself."

"That's sad."

"I know. He's on the computer constantly. He does Google Image search and puts Jonas' picture in to see if one pops up. He has joined this national database where police post pictures of individuals. Sadly, they said it could be weeks to update."

"Is it obsessive?" Jessie asked. "Should I be worried?"

"No, don't be worried and oh, yeah, it's obsessive. After these six weeks left in the semester, he's taking some time off."

"Dad is taking time off?"

Cate nodded. "He said if they find Jonas, he is going to dedicate that time to working with him. If we don't, then he is going out to look."

"Will you go with him?"

"I can't. I have my job at the home and that keeps my sanity. Plus," Cate said. "This may be something your dad needs to do on his own. His way of possibly working on his issues with his son. Looking for him, you know."

"We're going to find him, Mom," Jessie said. "One way or another."

"I know. I believe it. I do."

"Maybe we can convince Daddy."

Cate smiled gently and shook her head. "Him and Jonas are more alike than either of them want to admit. Both stubborn, both hot heads, and both of them don't listen. They have to see their own way, no one can show them."

"Mom, this may be far off," Jessie said. "Have you guys called rehabs?"

Cate paused in looking at the flowers. "Why do you say that?'

"It's an option. Maybe Jonas had a bad night last week, said enough is enough and checked himself in somewhere. I know it's hard to believe. Jonas is so narcissistic he wouldn't do that without announcing it to the world. But what if?"

"Then it would be the longest stint in rehab yet. He's never lasted more than a few days anywhere. I always said if he could go three weeks or a month, it could work. But in order for that to occur, your brother needs to find his purpose. Until that happens," Cate said. "He'll never find his way."

THIRTEEN

Pastor Rick had a lot of things going for him, but a green thumb was not one of them. His daughter, Haley suffered from the same 'lack of green thumb' affliction. It was his wife, Haley's mother, who had the talent.

Sadly, she had left them a few years earlier. Not by death, but by choice. She suddenly felt trapped, the church life wasn't for her and took she off for California. Pastor Rick and Haley had since resolved all conflict or hurt over it, even talked to her. But not about planting flowers.

"That's um …" Pastor Rick stood, hand on hips staring down. "Pretty sad."

"We tried," Haley replied.

"No, we didn't. Or not hard enough." He laughed, wrapping his arm around Haley. "I just don't have a love for this."

"Me either."

"Pastor Rick. Haley," Chief Russ' voice carried to them.

"Hi, Chief," Haley said.

"Chief." Pastor Rick took off his gardening glove and shook Russ' hand. "What brings you by?"

"Certainly not to look at the garden."

Pastor Rick grumbled then chuckled. "Some of us are put on the earth to help people, some for flowers. Flowers are not us. I'll bring it up at services tomorrow. Get a volunteer."

"Good. You always do. The reason for me being here. The accident victim formally known as Harold, now known as Chip is being released from the hospital as we speak."

"We know," Haley said. "Marge stopped by to get some clothes from the stash for the bazaar. She wanted to launder them. Is she getting him?"

"Yes, she is there now," Russ answered.

"Any luck with his identity?" Pastor Rick asked.

"None. I'm waiting to hear back from Harold, no return call yet. I checked all missing person data bases. Nothing. Call it a hunch. A father's hunch, but I think that young man may be bad news, and no one really wants to find him. At least, no one is looking for him right now. Not according to the national database."

"Doesn't that lag behind?" asked Pastor Rick.

"The national one, yeah. I reached out to Kansas State PD and Missouri. Since the car was from Kansas he has to be from that area."

"You would think," said Pastor Rick.

Haley shook her head. "This is so sad. What's gonna happen with him?"

"I talked to Amanda, the manager at the Hotel Six," Russ replied. "She said she'll give him a room. That won't help him eat or health wise. Truth is, he still doesn't know who he is. We don't know who he is. He is in our town. I can't help but feel a sense of responsibility. This town is like a big family. I'm not comfortable with the idea he is out there, lost in himself, no means to eat. You know. So, I was hoping Pastor you might, through the church, know of an organization. A shelter maybe, a place we could send him to find his way."

Pastor Rick nodded. "I do. I know exactly where he can go." He looked at Russ then Haley. "He survived that crash and ended up in our town. There's a reason for it. I think he should come here."

"Here?" Haley asked. "Dad. No."

"Why?"

"He's not that nice."

"Maybe that'll change," Pastor Rick said. "I haven't heard Marge say a bad thing about him."

"Maw-Maw wouldn't say a mean thing about anyone," Haley replied.

"You sure Pastor?" Russ asked.

"Absolutely." Pastor Rick nodded again. "We have that posting for a part time groundskeeper. I have that room. He can stay with me, work the church for his room and board. I am very sure."

Arms folded tightly, Haley exhaled and looked at the both of them. "I know what you guys are doing. And don't ..." She waved out her hand. "Don't say 'the right thing or the Christian thing', this goes beyond that. It's personal. You know it, I know it. Just remember, trying to save this lost soul is not going to make up for the lost soul you couldn't save."

"You're right. But we can try, can't we?" Pastor Rick leaned forward and kissed his daughter on the forehead. "We can try."

It had been nearly twenty-four hours since Marge had seen him and what a difference that time had made in the young man she called Chip. He sat on a bench in the small hospital park. A bag of belongings on his lap. Probably the ones she dropped off for him. He wore blue jeans and a crisp white tee shirt. His face was still very bruised, but the swelling had gone down, and his hair was shorter. Very short, parted on the side with a little flip added to the front like the boy bands used to do. He looked ... clean cut.

Carrying a takeout container, Marge walked to him. "Look at you. Betty, the hospital beautician, got her hands on someone today."

"Doc Jenner said it was a fresh look for a fresh start."

"And you agreed?" Marge asked.

He nodded, running his hand over the top of his hair.

"I like it."

"It's not me."

"We don't know that," Marge said. "Hey, it matches the name Chip." She handed him the container. "For you."

"Food?" He lifted the lid. "Wow, Nachos, thank you. You always bring me food. Ann said I gained six pounds this week."

"Yep, fourteen more will make me happy. Eat."

He dipped into his snack.

"Chief Russ tells me you declined a fingerprint search. Can I ask why?"

He nodded. "Yeah, I um ... well, if I match that means I have a record."

"Okay."

"Chances are, I probably do. I mean, someone drugged me, at least it's what Doc Jenner said. So, I probably did something to make someone mad."

"People do things and don't need a reason. You don't know," she said.

"One of those feelings." He glanced up at her, then looked down to his food. "I just ... it may sound strange to you, but I want to try to have my memory come back and know who I am rather than someone tell me, and I have to make myself fit the narrative. Like I tried to do when they said I was Harold."

Marge nodded. "I see. I can tell you one thing about yourself. You're intelligent. No one says 'fits the narrative' unless they're a writer or big reader. But declining the fingerprints is your choice and I think you have the right attitude."

"I was thinking of giving myself a time frame."

"You can do that," she said. "Or see what happens. Up to you. How are you feeling?"

"Good."

"Any memories?"

"I get feelings. Like I told you about. Feelings about things I like or want."

"Like what?" Marge asked.

"I think I was a smoker. I keep feeling like I want a cigarette. And pot roast. It's like I feel like pot roast is something I like."

"Well, lucky you, Pot Roast is my Sunday supper."

"There you go feeding me again."

Marge laughed. "That's just me. We can go on these feelings.

They have to be helpful. Still, no memories?

"Of my life? No." He shook his head. "But of that night I do, I still see his face."

"David's?"

"Yes. His face telling me, 'I got you'. Do you think he's dead?"

"I don't know. There are some folks who don't think a man was in the car with you."

"Like I'm nuts."

"No." She shook her head. "Not nuts. Don't use that word. They believe you weren't alone."

"They don't believe a man was in the car, but they don't think I was alone ..." Then it hit him. "You mean, like they think it was God that was riding with me?"

"Some folks feel that way. Old Joe does."

"Hmm. Interesting."

"Wow, no scoffing. I'm shocked."

"Another feeling ... I feel like usually I would scoff," he said. "But I really think whoever was in the car with me is a key to a lot. I can't put my finger on it. I keep thinking that once I figure him out, I can figure me out. A key."

"A key to your survival that night? Your new journey."

He chuckled. "Is that why you're here Maw-Maw, to take me to wherever I am going?"

"I am." Marge nodded. "I am your driver. You can't just be discharged from the hospital, Chip, with only a good riddance. You don't know who you are and you're still healing. You landed right smack in Williams Peak. You couldn't ask for a better place. We take care of our own and right now, you are one of our own. Until you figure out who you are. Until you find your way, we have a place for you."

"Where?"

"You'll find out shortly." Marge tapped his food container. "Eat your nachos."

◆ ◆ ◆

Jonas just stared at the room, taking in the simplicity of it. Everything in the town was simplistic. The room had a twin bed which was in the corner of the room. A window on each wall was by it. There was a television on a desk and a dresser.

It was a room in Pastor Rick's home. The two story, white frame building directly across the street from the church.

Maw-Maw, Pastor Rick and Haley were crowded by the door. He supposed they were waiting for him to say something.

"You don't ..." Pastor Rick stepped to him. "Have to stay here or take the job. We just thought it would be good for you. Once you're on your feet, know who you are, it's up to you then. Who knows? You may even stay in Williams Peak."

Jonas turned around. "I doubt I am the type of person that lives in a town like this. But, as Maw-Maw always says, I don't know, because I don't remember."

"You'll take it?" Pastor Rick asked. "As I said, we can call the Motel Six. They offered you a room there, the chief is working on finding out who you are ..."

"No." Jonas shook his head. "This is great. What will I be doing? I'm not sure I have any skills. If I do, I don't remember them."

"We'll all help you," Pastor Rick said. "Help me take care of the church, put the books out for service. Help set up for music rehearsals, stuff like that."

Maw-Maw added, "We have the bazaar in six days. On Friday, and we will need some help with that."

"It'll add a few bucks in your pocket, not much," Pastor Rick said. "A roof over your head and food. I'm a great cook."

Haley cleared her throat.

Jonas quickly looked at her.

"What?" Pastor Rick asked. "I'm a great cook. And you'll find out shortly." He waved his finger at Jonas. "Lunch is in a few minutes, Chip. Marge, lend me a hand?"

"Absolutely." She and the pastor walked out.

"So ... was this your room?" Jonas asked Haley.

"It was. We grabbed some things from the donated bazaar items. My dad had this crazy idea to make this his exercise room after I moved out. But that never happened."

"How long ago did you move out?" Jonas asked.

"Six years ago. I have a place in town near my job. I work at the veterinary clinic."

"Oh, you don't work here?"

"I do that, too."

"I didn't see your mom. Does she live here?" Jonas asked.

Haley shook her head. "She lives in California, teaching high school or something. Long story. I'll tell you all about it one day. As for right now." She walked toward the door. "You're about to experience my dad's cooking."

"I'm sure it's fine. Everyone is trying to feed me."

"That's because you're so thin," she said. "And that didn't happen because of the car accident." She paused in the doorway. "Hey, Chip. I'm sorry you and I got off on the wrong foot the day we met."

"Why are you apologizing to me?" he asked. "I wasn't very nice."

"No, you weren't, but it wasn't my place to call you out like I did."

"Someone had to."

"Yep. But that's Maw-Maw's place. She has a way of doing it without you knowing it. Trust me."

"I know."

"Lunch?"

"Yeah." He walked to the door, pausing to look back at the room before he left.

Jonas couldn't decipher how he felt about it all, the room, the job, the town he accidentally arrived in. It was hard to figure out how he felt about anything, when he couldn't even figure out who he was.

FOURTEEN

The squad car was parked curbside directly in front of the walking path to the church. Marge knew it was the Chief's car, his name was on it. She was curious when she saw it, she couldn't recall seeing the Chief ever at the church. Surely, he wasn't there for services, a quick in and out of some sorts. Not even the chief would be so brazen as to block the main walkway to the church right before the eleven am service.

As she made it up the path, the chief was walking out. He nodded to the church goers as he passed them and stopped before Marge.

"Well, hello there, Chief. This is a surprise. Are you checking up on Chip?"

"I'm going to. I heard he's on the side of the church working on the flower beds."

"Oh, boy, Pastor Rick will just let anyone touch those flowers. I knew there had to be some reason for seeing you here."

"I'm here every Sunday," Russ replied. "You go to this contemporary service; I go to the traditional. The coffee at the mingle is much fresher." He held up his obnoxious cheese curl designed travel mug.

"Oh, so you only stop by for the coffee."

"Pastor Rick likes to keep the law caffeinated."

Marge smiled. "Go check on Chip, and make sure he ate. That boy is still skin and bones."

"I'm sure he ate. Rick always boasts he starts out his day with a hearty breakfast."

"From a freezer box."

"Breakfast is breakfast, Marge. Go to church." He placed a

hand on her shoulder and gave her a nod.

Marge walked ahead to the church, alone, without her husband Old Joe.

Joe stopped going to church not long before. Russ understood why. Old Joe had his reasons for not going, he just hadn't found his reason to go back.

Sipping the refreshed coffee, he got from the contemporary service mingle, Russ walked around to the side of the building.

He didn't really know what to expect, he just knew not to expect much.

Pastor Rick told him he sent Chip out to work the flower beds on the side of the building. The kid didn't know his name, how in the world was he to even remember gardening?

Russ was wrong.

He hadn't seen the flower bed look so wonderful, not since the Pastor's former wife tended to it.

Chip was on his hands and knees, planting what looked like the last batch of annuals.

"Will you look at this," Russ said. "Did you remember how to do this?"

"Actually, no," he replied. "Pastor asked if I wanted to fiddle with it. He told me to start on the side that way if I messed up no one would see."

"You didn't mess up."

"My hands just took over."

"Did you have one of those memory feelings?"

"Once I started it, it was automatic." He glanced over his shoulder. "Then I just didn't …"

Russ waited. Chip just paused. "Are you alright?"

"Your coffee mug."

"My daughter got this for me. Ugly isn't it?"

"It seems familiar. I don't know why. The pattern. The cheese curl pattern is just …I've seen it. I know it."

"Maybe you have one." Russ held it up. "Or a love of cheese curls."

"Maybe." He chuckled.

"Keep up the good work. Pastor Rick is going to be proud. That's impressive. Are you … are you going into service?"

"Me?" he scoffed. "No. No. I heard the organ music and mass choir style singing earlier. Not for me."

"Oh, this service is the rock band."

"Rock band?" he asked. "A church rock band."

"Well, not rock. The older folks call it noise," Russ explained. "Pastor Rick is still hoping it will be the draw. Bring younger folks in from other towns around here, he kept telling the church counsel over and over it will pack the house."

"It hasn't?"

"Hmm. Not yet. All it will take is one good Sunday. I believe that," Russ said. "Word spreads fast in these parts. I'm gonna head out on patrol. I think the front of the church should be your next move."

"I'll tell Pastor Rick. Have a good day, Chief."

Hearing him say that as he walked away, gave Russ pause. "Yes, thank you, Chip. You as well."

As he walked away, he looked back at the newcomer. The young man with the slightly bruised face and boy band haircut.

He came into town screaming and angry. It had been one week since that accident, and already he saw a change in the young man. It could be short lived or the fact that he couldn't remember anymore why he was so angry. Whatever the reason, Russ was starting to think for the young man's sake, maybe it wasn't such a bad idea after all to encourage him to stay in town.

Jonas had no intention whatsoever of going into the church. He had his fill after just hearing the sounds of the morning service. It made him tired. But the second he heard the drums, something kicked in him. And it wasn't just the overly loud bass drum.

He was curious. Was there a drummer in there practicing or

did it sound differently inside than it did out?

Something about the sound of the music pulled him, and he didn't know why.

He thought he could slip in the back of the church unnoticed and listen. Perhaps because the music called to him so much it would trigger something.

His thought of being unnoticed went out the window when he saw there were only a couple dozen people in the church. Unlike earlier where he saw hundreds of people walking in.

Jonas didn't remember much, but he was certain his dirty tee-shirt and 'I was just digging in the dirt' look wasn't church appropriate.

He stayed in the back and watched. There was a drummer, a couple of guitar players and an older woman singing.

Those in attendance tried to follow along, looking at the screen for words that were totally mismatched from what the worship leader sang.

He spotted Maw-Maw a few rows up. Then as if she had some sort of radar on him, she looked back and over her shoulder.

She smiled and waved for him to come join her.

Jonas shook his head.

She had this insistent look and he relented and walked to her.

She grinned at him and scooted over.

"I'm not dressed for this," Jonas whispered.

"No one cares," she replied. "Here." She handed him a program. "Sing."

"No. It's off."

"I know. They try. God love them. They're pouring their hearts into this. Look at them."

Jonas did. He could see it on their faces, they were feeling, singing praise. But he couldn't hear it. The drums drowned out everything. He couldn't distinguish one guitar from the other and if the singers were singing in tune, Jonas wouldn't know.

He didn't understand why, but it stirred an antsy feeling in his gut. He didn't understand why he felt so upset that it sounded so wrong.

It was missing its point. Music was supposed to move and inspire, but it was distracting. At least to him.

"Maw-Maw, who is running how this sounds?" Jonas asked.

"What do you mean?"

"Someone has to be controlling what we're hearing."

"Oh, I don't think anyone is controlling it," she said. "Pastor Rick sets everything back there." She turned and pointed to the back of the church where an older man stood back with folded arms.

"Is that a security guard?"

Marge laughed. "No, that's Burgess he's just keeping an eye out. I don't know why. It might be the mixing center. I don't know the technical stuff. Don't worry about it, Chip." She patted his hand. "They're all learning."

Jonas looked at the band, then back at Burgess. Again, he felt this 'drawn' feeling and he slipped from the row.

"Chip," Marge whispered his name. "What are you doing?"

Jonas lifted a finger to her mouthing the words, 'I'll be back' and walked straight toward Burgess.

When he arrived back there, he saw what Burgess was standing by. A table that held a large music mixing board and a small laptop computer. He could see the words to the song scrolling, they seemed to be about three seconds faster than what the band on stage played.

Burgess had his arms folded as if he was conveying, "I'm not touching this.'

Jonas approached him. "You know if you pull back the drums, it will sound better."

"What do you mean pull back the drums?"

"I don't know," Jonas replied. "I don't even know why I used that term." His eyes shifted to the gear on the table. "Can I?"

"Oh, I don't care. Pastor Rick may get mad, but if you know what you're doing, go for it"

That was the point, Jonas didn't know if he knew what he was doing.

He looked at the large board. Sliding levers with a row of turning knobs above each lever. They were labeled as well. Drums one, bass drum, snare drum, lead guitar and so forth.

Every level was the exact same including the microphone for the singers.

The first thing Jonas did was look at the laptop. He reached over and hit the spacebar, pausing the scrolling words. He didn't know the song, not at all, but he listened and hit the spacebar again to restart it. It wasn't a close match to what the band sang, but it was better.

Swept over by one of those memory feelings, and not understanding how or what he knew, Jonas took a seat behind the mixing board.

Following that 'Feeling' Jonas started moving levers, turning knobs on high ends, low ends, mids...

It took until the beginning of the third song and things clicked. It was like a puzzle he had to solve, pressing buttons, changing things until it sounded right.

"Chip?" He heard Haley's voice right behind him. She actually sounded panicked. "Chip. What are you doing?"

Jonas froze, his hands slowly lifted, he closed his eyes for a moment and turned around. "I'm sorry, Haley. I don't know why I... I'll stop."

"No." She shook her head. "I was going to say, whatever you're doing, keep going. That sounds amazing. Thank you."

"Really."

"Yes. Pay attention." She pointed to the board, then stood next to him.

"Something tells me if I knew the songs, I could even do this better."

"We're gonna have to change that then. But for now ..." She pointed down to the board. "Just keep it up."

Jonas smiled at her. He honestly didn't know how he was doing it, or even what he was doing. He was following that feeling, following the sound, and it just felt right.

FIFTEEN

Jonas wished he knew if he ever felt in his life as appreciated as he did that moment after the contemporary service, when everyone told him what a difference it made the second he jumped in to work the controls.

"Finally," someone told him. "We could hear the pastor. I thought he had a toothache or something before."

Then again, Jonas didn't remember anything, technically, it *was* the first time in his life he could recall feeling so good.

With that came a new job.

Pastor Rick asked if he would work the board for services and rehearsals. But Jonas had to learn the songs a little better and the program that projected the words on a screen from a laptop that was running on an outdated operating system.

They used the pastor's office because he had an extensive library of music plus, he subscribed to one of those unlimited music plans.

Haley told Jonas he reminded her of those 'Reaction' videos she always watched online.

He didn't know what they were, and she explained that it was videos of people listening to a different type of music or song they had never heard. She loved watching someone just freak with joy. Not that Jonas was freaking with joy, but he had reacted a lot according to her.

He didn't think he did. The music didn't sound shocking to him, so much so he was convinced at some point he had been exposed to it.

"What do you think?" Haley asked. "It's older, but one of my favorites."

"Is this all you listen to?" Jonas asked.

"What? Do you mean like is Christian music all I have on my playlist?"

"Yeah."

"No, I like country and old boy band stuff. Though I have to say your haircut took me back."

Jonas grumbled a 'thanks'.

"You know I've been thinking," she said. "The way you naturally went to the mixing board. I wonder if you were a DJ coming home from a gig. I mean, I can't explain the gardening, but if you think about it. It was late and ... there's a rave outside of Lincoln. Raves are notorious for people slipping stuff into people's drinks."

"That's actually a good theory," Jonas said.

"How does it feel to you? Does it ring a bell?"

"Not really. Though I'm kind of stuck on the fact that you just told me there is a rave in Lincoln, Nebraska. It's almost like an oxymoron."

Haley laughed, then turned her head when there was a knock on the arch of the door.

"Dinner is just about done," Pastor Rick said.

"Dad? Isn't it early?" Haley asked.

"Ping pong league starts back up tonight," he said. "How's it going? You've been at this for a couple days."

Jonas answered, "I want to be ready for rehearsal tomorrow night. Who picks the songs?"

He lifted his hand. "Me. I do. I pick them. You can't just select a song because it's good, you have to pick the music to match the message. Like this coming Sunday it will be about giving it to God. I try to touch that message at least once a year; people tend to forget."

"I see." Jonas nodded. "You pick songs that deal with handing it over. Got it."

"Yes, and the following week I have a 'God is First' theme."

"You can do like a 'He not Me' theme and do all songs that start with He, because there are a ton of them."

Pastor Rick smiled. "Chip, that's really clever. Very clever."

"Have you ever picked your sermon and message based on a song you heard?'

"No."

"Why?"

"I … I don't know, that's not how it works."

"Christian music is meant to inspire and move, at least that's what Haley told me," Jonas said. "Why don't you have it one day inspire and move you to a message?"

"I … I don't know. We'll see. Right now. Dinner. I ran two towns over to get that rotisserie chicken from Costco and you can only reheat it once before it dries out. Haley, are you staying?"

"Um …" she stammered in her answer. "You know what? Yes. I will stay. It will save me from having to cook for myself. Then I have to go. It's a long day tomorrow. I have to work, then back here. We have deliveries, teen group, evening rehearsal, and I have to try to get the cemetery visits in, and by myself it will take a while."

Pastor Rick said, "I can do the cemetery thing."

"No, Daddy you can't," she said. "You have hospital visits in Fremont."

"I can help," Jonas said, as he stood from behind the desk. "With whatever you need. I mean, I work here, right."

Pastor Rick nodded. "Yes, you can. Right now that chicken is calling us and since I'll be in Fremont tomorrow, I'll grab those frozen raviolis from Walmart you like so much, Haley."

Haley just gave a closed mouth smile as her father walked out of the office. "Yum."

"It's not that bad," Jonas said.

"Oh, what do you know, you can't remember if you ever had a fast food burger."

"True. What's this cemetery thing?"

"We go to the local cemetery, there's about six people who went to our church that passed that don't have family, so we go once a week and try to make the graves look nice. And yes, you volunteered for that."

"That uh … sounds interesting."

"Not as interesting as those ravioli you have to eat tomorrow." Haley walked toward the door. "Oh, hey, put that on pause so you remember where you left off."

He thought at first that she was making a memory joke about forgetting where he left off, then he realized she was being serious about the tracks he was listening to. He returned to the desk, leaned down, grabbed the mouse and as he clicked it, he saw the title of the song. 'I got you'

Jonas froze when he read those words. They sent something through him, the title to the song were the words spoken and only memory of that night.

More than anything he wanted to immediately listen to that song, but he knew he had chicken waiting for him and the song would still be there later.

It wasn't the song that did it to him, it was the title. How many times over the last week and a half since the accident, did he see that face and hear that voice.

"I got you."

In fact, Jonas never really listened to the song. He didn't press play at all. After dinner and after Haley left to go home and Pastor Rick went to his ping pong league, Jonas retreated to the office to listen.

He sat down, put on the headphones, reached for the mouse and his eyes just stayed on those words.

That was when it happened.

Flashes of memories, not feelings like he had been getting, but memories. He knew they were memories. Pieces of a puzzle, snippets. It was like watching a trailer to a movie, no substance, no explanation and possibly misleading.

He couldn't count on them being in the order they had happened because he could see his own bloody hand reaching out from that broken windshield.

"I got you," David's face appeared. *"I'm here."*

Then he was back in a moving car, looking at David in the passenger seat.

"Do you think you could have turned the other cheek?" David said.

"I did," His own voice spoke in the memory. *"He punched it."*

Punched? Who? Who punched him?

"Who are you?"

"David."

"What do you want?"

David's face zoomed in close in that memory. "I thought I'd take this ride with you."

Then the memory went blurry, it was almost hard to decipher what he was seeing. But he remembered, he heard David's voice.

"Denying it isn't the answer. Admitting the truth is the first step to righting a wrong and to setting you on a new path."

"Deer."

Crash.

"I got you."

Done.

Jonas flung off the headset and jumped from his seat.

He was suddenly flooded with memories of this stranger, the passenger in his car. A man who spoke with wisdom.

A man who told him "I thought I'd take this ride with you."

That short but powerful series of memories of the crash frightened Jonas some, and he knew exactly who he needed to talk to.

He walked briskly three blocks down and two streets over. It wasn't late. The sun was just starting to set. In that phase where once it went down it was dark in the snap of a finger. Jonas was certain she wasn't sleeping, and he could see the porch light was already on when he approached.

Old Joe was sitting on the porch in one of those nice, padded porch chairs. He was eating watermelon and just staring out, until he caught sight of Jonas headed his way.

Old Joe lifted his hand and waved as Jonas approached the porch.

"Hey there, what brings you over?"

"Mr. Baker is Maw-Maw here?" Jonas stood, one foot on the first step.

He set his plate on the table next to the empty chair beside him. "No, sorry, Chip, she's baking tonight."

"Oh. Alright, thanks."

"Everything all right?"

"Yeah, I wanted to talk to her."

"Is Pastor Rick not home?" Old Joe asked.

"He's at Ping Pong, but I guess I just feel more comfortable talking to Maw-Maw."

"Most people do," Joe said.

"I know. I had some memories about the crash, they're not all clear and, well, can you tell her I stopped by?"

"Sure thing."

Jonas stepped back.

Old Joe stood. "Chip, you know I am here. You can bounce them off of me. If something is bothering you, or whatever, I wouldn't mind at all, in fact, I'd like to talk to you. I remember that night. It was a scary night."

It wasn't that Jonas didn't trust or like Old Joe, that wasn't it. He knew there was a safety factor with Maw-Maw, a no judgment, yet honest zone. However, Jonas needed to talk, he was afraid if he didn't speak his thoughts of the memories out loud he'd forget or distort them somehow.

"If you don't mind," Jonas said.

"Not at all. Have a seat." He patted the chair next to him. "Watermelon?"

"No thank you." Jonas sat down. The chair was comfortable, and he sank into it.

"That there," Joe said. "Is a talking chair. Maw-Maw sits in it and doesn't stop chatting."

Jonas laughed.

"Now, let's talk."

"I had flashes of memories from that night. Sights, sounds, it wasn't a long stream of the entire accident, but flashes. But they weren't the memory feelings I have been getting."

"Memory feelings?" Joe asked.

"It's like I feel it, I sense something, but I can't remember if it's true. An example is the memory feeling I have about being a smoker. I can't remember smoking. It just feels like I enjoy cigarettes."

"Oh, you were a smoker," Joe said.

"How do you know?"

"I could smell it on you when you were in my car."

"Maw-Maw didn't say anything."

"She probably didn't notice or remember. I noticed it because it immediately made me think of someone. Like ..." he lifted the plate. "Watermelon makes you think of summer."

"Oh, wow, cool, thank you. That just validated my memory feelings."

"See. I can be a good one to talk to. So how much of the accident did you remember?"

"Not much. We hit a deer. I don't remember seeing it, but he told me."

"He? The passenger in the car with you?" Joe asked.

"He said to call him David. Most of what was flashing to me was about him. And we talked, but I can't remember the context of it., I told him I had been punched. I can't remember when or why. But it was a reply to something he said."

"Which was?"

"He asked why I didn't turn the other cheek."

"Hmm." Joe leaned back in his chair. "Then you were probably discussing something which happened that night."

"I think so. I could feel in those memories I was so angry. So very angry and uptight. Yet, he was being calm and saying things that were just ... this is gonna sound weird. He was profound."

"In what way?"

"He said something about having to admit the truth so I can get on the right path. He said ... Mr. Baker, when I asked what he wanted he said he was there to take the ride with me. Then the accident happened, then I saw him. I saw him outside that busted windshield. He said he had me, and he was there, and that was all I remembered until I woke up in the hospital."

"You're saying this out loud, you're wanting to talk to Marge because in your mind, it has this idea."

"Yes, it does."

"Let me say this." Joe leaned forward. "A lot of folks, including myself, don't think there was a person like you or me in that car with you. Hence why they haven't found a body. And if you remember him being outside the windshield, they aren't gonna find that body. Either he is one lucky person and ran away for some reason or ... you weren't riding alone in that car, son. Marge will tell you, one way or another, Jesus was riding in the car with you. I think, and this is just me, he was, and he said his name was David."

"It doesn't make sense."

"Yes, it does. Think about it. Think about the things he said. He got you. He's there. Turn the other cheek. He's taking the ride with you. Then gone, disappeared, nowhere to be found. He knew you were in trouble that night. Like they say we don't walk alone, well, Chip, you didn't drive alone."

"Why me?" Jonas asked.

"Why not you?"

"Because I don't know, I'm not worthy. A memory or feeling, Mr. Baker tells me I just ...if I was all that worthy, why was I so angry?"

"First." Joe held up a finger. "We're all worthy. Second, maybe you were angry, not just about that night, but at life itself. Angry because you didn't like yourself, and didn't like your choices. I knew someone like that. They hated the world because they hated themselves. God loves us all, faults and all. Maybe He has a plan for you. Maybe that was why He put His son in the car with you that night."

"Just to save my life? I mean why save my life and then have me not remember it?"

"All part of a plan. You forgot everything, right? But you didn't forget the passenger in your car. To me that speaks volumes. You remembered what you were supposed to. Let me ask you this. Would it be all that bad to just go on the assumption that He was in the car with you? That you were given a chance? Your memory is gone so you can see through fresh eyes? To walk the walk, He may want you to? Would that be so bad?"

"No, Mr. Baker it wouldn't."

"It's worth giving it a try. In my opinion, I also think once you accept who your passenger really was and what He did for you, you'll find your path and remember." He reached over and lifted the plate. "Now, have some watermelon because my wife will give me all kinds of grief if she finds out I didn't feed you."

Jonas smiled and grabbed a slice of watermelon. "Thank you. And … thank you for being there that night."

"More than you realize, Chip, I'm glad I was there."

Jonas brought the watermelon near his mouth. He could feel the juice run down his fingers. He was really glad he had talked to Old Joe. He felt better.

The conversation, the porch, Old Joe, Jonas was glad he happened to end up in Williams Peak. Eventually he would learn the reason, until then, Old Joe gave him not only that slice of watermelon and wisdom, but maybe the direction he needed to take.

SIXTEEN

Russ figured, 'why not', when Pastor Rick asked if he wanted to take the ride into Fremont with him. Pastor Rick knew how much Russ enjoyed going to Fremont. And since Russ' wife never liked to take the short drive, Russ went there whenever he could. A lot of people from Williams Peak went there to get things they needed to avoid the bigger city.

It was Russ' day off and Fremont had a lot of great things about it. They had that Super Walmart, and you could go to Fridays Restaurant for lunch. Russ loved Fridays. His go to eatery in Fremont used to be the Ponderosa Steak House. It was actually one of the last remaining Ponderosa's in the country.

There was a good bit Russ could do to pass time while the Pastor did his hospital visits.

One place in particular was Guitar World. It sold everything and anything that had to do with music. Not that Russ knew how to play any instrument, but he enjoyed looking at the things. And on this day, he was more inspired to go. During the drive, his friend gushed about how good the contemporary service was going to be, especially after they obtained what they needed. Russ was inspired. Pastor Rick rambled on about the problems they faced, what the contemporary band needed, and what they'd eventually get once their budget allowed.

That's when Russ had the idea he'd get a little gift for the church. His contribution. It wouldn't be the first time Russ had got a gift for the church, nor would it be the last. It wasn't out of the ordinary, but it was the first time he was flying blind on what to get.

The baby Jesus for the life size nativity scene was pretty specific, as were the advent calendars to give to each kid in Sunday school. For this, Russ was only armed with the information Pastor Rick had given him.

The guy in Guitar World looked like he was still in high school, but more than likely he wasn't. Everyone looked young to Russ. He wanted to get one of the older, seasoned workers, but they were all busy.

The teen looking clerk was really attentive, nodding and putting on a face that said he was listening.

"I'm stuck," Russ said. "I want to get something for the contemporary band, but I just don't know what."

"Okay, so you don't play?"

"No."

"You don't even go to the church?"

Russ shook his head.

"But you want to help, and you know the drums are loud, there's no keyboard playing."

"They have someone to play, but only the organist Miss Milly."

The young man cringed some. "Organ has its place, dude, not sure it works with contemporary worship."

"Yes. That's what I was told. Any suggestions?"

"Yeah, we'll get you a keyboard and we can do a drum shield."

"What is that?" Russ asked.

"Kind of like sound proofs the drums."

"Perfect."

"What kind of keyboard?" the clerk asked.

"Something inexpensive but not cheap."

"All right let's look at the boards." He gave a wave of his hand for Russ to follow him.

Russ did, looking around as he walked. "You know I always wanted to play."

"Never too late to learn. I can see you holding a sweet acoustic."

Russ chuckled, then stopped when he saw it. It screamed

at him, caught his eye, and not because it was something he wanted to buy. Something about it turned on his police instincts immediately.

"You like it?" the clerk asked. "We figured it was custom made."

Russ stared at the electric guitar. The design across the front was cheese curls and eerily similar to his obnoxious travel mug.

Immediately his mind went back to a few days earlier when he watched Chip fixing the garden.

"Are you alright?" Russ had asked him when he noticed Chip went into this 'deer in the headlights' stare.

"Your coffee mug."

"My daughter got this for me. Ugly, isn't it?"

"It seems familiar. I don't know why. The pattern. The cheese curl pattern is just …I've seen it. I know it."

"Maybe you have one. Or a love of cheese curls."

It was completely possible Chip had jumped to that sound board because he was a musician but didn't remember.

Russ pointed to it. "Custom made meaning what?"

The clerk shook his head. "Someone had this made and picked this pattern."

"So, this is used. How long have you had it?"

"Not even a week. Not sure the guy who brought it in was even a guitar player. Sold it really cheap to us."

"Were you the one?" Russ asked. "Did you buy it from him?"

"No, our manager did."

"Is he around?"

"No, he's off today."

Russ reached into his back pocket, removed his wallet and pulled out a business card. He handed it to the young clerk. "Could you give this to him and have him call me. I would like information about the guy who brought that in."

The clerk read the card. "Whoa, chief of police in Williams Peak."

"Yeah. We have an accident victim, amnesia. I think he may be a musician and something he said the other day about cheese curls looking familiar. I may be way off. Who knows?"

"I'll give this to the manager."

"I appreciate it. Now, let's look at those keyboards."

The young clerk led the way again. Not only did Russ look once more at the guitar, but he also pulled out his phone and took a picture.

◆ ◆ ◆

"Thomas Walters." Haley hunched down by the tomb stone and pulled some weeds. "He was a veteran. A really nice man. He used to come to the fish fry to help for as long as I can remember."

Jonas did the math on the tombstone. Thomas was eighty-nine when he passed away.

"And you do this every week?"

Haley nodded.

"I don't understand why," Jonas said. "Don't take this the wrong way, but Thomas doesn't know."

"We do. Cemeteries are memorials to those we lost. When there's no family around someone has to keep that memory alive, this is our way of doing it."

"Did you ever not want to be so nice?"

Haley laughed. "What?"

"You're nice."

"No, I'm not that nice."

"Yes, you are. Your dad, even the chief. Everyone is so nice. But you're young, do you ever feel like just being bad?"

"Bad? Like?"

"Go out, have some drinks ..."

"That's not being bad as long as you don't overdo it," Haley said. "It's not a sin or bad to drink, the sin is to overindulge. And to answer your question, no. When you're fulfilled in life and happy, you don't need to do things that aren't good. At least that's my opinion. Why are you asking this, do you feel like being bad? Is that calling you?"

"It's not that. No, it's …" Jonas turned his head and paused.

"Chip?"

"Marge," he spoke softly. How did he miss her? She was fifty or so feet away, sat on what looked like a marble bench, her back was to Jonas. "Can you excuse me? I'll be right back."

"Sure. But Chip, she may want to be alone."

"I understand. I just want …" he pointed, then turned and walked over to Marge.

She never heard him coming.

"Maw-Maw?" Jonas called her name.

"Oh, hey, Chip."

"Are you alright?"

"Hmm. Yes."

"I saw you and wanted to check on you."

"You can sit if you want." She patted the spot next to her.

"I will." As soon as Jonas sat down, he saw the headstone.

Matthew Baker.

He was thirty-one.

Jonas looked at Marge.

"My son, Matt. We lost him a year ago today."

"I … I didn't know. I'm so sorry."

"I'm sorry, too."

"I'll leave you be."

"No, Chip, stay." She reached over laying her hand on his. "More than you know, I'm glad you are here. I'm … glad you stopped and talked to Joe last night."

"He was really helpful."

"Good. I'm glad." She sighed out and looked at the grave. "I can't believe it's been a year. It feels like only yesterday he was looking in the fridge for something to eat. You know … when we met, the first moment I saw you, you reminded me so much of him."

"We look alike?"

"Oh, no." She shook her head. "Aside from being thin. It was the lost look in your eyes, the cry for help that seeped from you.

And I don't mean just from the accident."

"I know what you mean," Jonas said. "I get the feeling I wasn't a very good person."

"No. We're all good people, we just make bad choices. Choices which can cost us dearly. Matt ... Matt struggled with choices. He was ..." she glanced at Jonas. "Struggling with demons. He liked 'the drink', he had his substance issues. Didn't matter how much we loved him or wanted to help, he did his thing. One night, he argued with us again and took off. That was the last time we heard from him. They found him on a side of a hill near Fremont. He had fallen, broken his femur, and passed out from too much drink and blood loss, died there alone."

Jonas closed his eyes. "Oh, Maw-Maw, I am sorry."

"It hurts you know. To think of him alone out there. But he's at peace now. I know it. He's not fighting those demons anymore." She squeezed Jonas' hand. "When you happened upon our town, everyone wanted to help you. I especially wanted to help you. I kept looking at you and thinking, 'this boy has a mother out there whose heart is broken because she doesn't know where he is.' And I made a vow, no matter how angry or nasty you were, for her, you would be fed, clothed, warmed and cared for. You would not be alone."

A lump formed in Jonas' throat. "Thank you."

"You have a family out there, Chip, you may not know who you are, but they do. They'll find you. They love you that much."

"Then for their sake, I need to do the right thing. I need to make sure I'm on the right path, because I don't think I was."

"One of those memory feelings?" she asked.

Jonas nodded. "Yeah. A big one, I'm learning a lot here. I'm scared, I'm scared to find out who I am."

"Correction, who you were. You're scared to find out who you were. I think you're finding out who you are truly, the only thing you need to remember," She smiled at him. "Is your name."

◆ ◆ ◆

They came in through the rear entrance of the church. A single glass door that was a back way into her father's office. Haley didn't want to walk through the church with a milkshake in her hand. Not when there were nine teenagers waiting on her.

She set the keys on the bookshelf in her father's office. "Like I said, Chip, you might want to leave that milkshake here. Those kids will make you feel guilty for having it. They'll just stare."

Jonas laughed. "I'll leave it here." He took one more drink and set it on the bookshelf, as well.

"You sure you want to join teen group today?"

"What's the difference between teen group and youth group?"

"Age. This group is older." She pulled the office door closed.

"What are we doing with them?" Jonas asked, walking with her toward the sanctuary. "I mean, what are you doing with them?"

"Milly is supposed to be here for the sing along, then we talk about scripture that applies to their lives and have pizza."

"Ah, Milly is the eighty year old organ player?"

"That's right."

"They're going to sing along with an organ player?"

"Beggars can't be choosers." She stepped into the church. The teenagers were sitting in the pews waiting. Bright and almost too bubbly, Haley called out. "Hey everyone, sorry I'm late. I'm surprised you haven't ..." she looked over to the organ. "Milly isn't here yet either?"

One of the teen boys answered, "Not yet."

"Well, no wonder you haven't started singing. This ..." she waved out her hand. "Is Chip, my friend, he'll be joining us today. He's running sound for the contemporary service now. And I thought ..." Haley's head turned at the long ring of a service bell. "That must be the delivery. Chip, can you take over?"

"What ... what am I supposed to do?"

"I don't know. Tell them about your accident. I'll be right back." She darted off.

Awkwardly, Jonas faced the group. "Well."

A teenage girl raised her hand. "Are you the guy that survived the Broke Man's curve crash?"

"I am. Yeah."

Another girl raised her hand. "I heard Jesus was in the car with you."

"There was someone in the car with me."

Another spoke up, "So, you're saying you don't believe God was in the car with you?"

"That's not what I'm saying, I am just ..." Jonas looked around and he froze when he saw the acoustic guitar on the stand. The guitar player must have dropped it off ahead of rehearsal. Instantly, Jonas wondered why he would do that. He was drawn to it and walked over.

"Do you play?" someone asked.

"I don't know. I don't remember much about myself." He lifted it. The moment he slung the strap over his head and the neck of the instrument rested in his left hand, it felt right.

Natural.

Without even thinking about it, without knowing why or how he would know to do it, Jonas immediately checked the tuning of the guitar. He pressed the low E string on the fifth fret, matching it to the open A string, repeating to make sure the tones matched up. He did it quickly, because the guitar was in tune and Jonas strummed a chord to finish.

"I guess I do," he said and smiled. "How about that?"

"Play something."

He couldn't think of a single song he knew, if fact he wouldn't know the chords or did he? Jonas just started playing. "I'm supposed to tell you about my accident ... somehow, I know this song. I don't think I wrote it." He joked. "Let's see how this goes."

"Right there, thank you," Haley instructed the delivery driver on where to place the box. She had him set it right inside her Father's office. She snuck a sip of her shake, set it down and took the clipboard he handed to her. "I appreciate you carrying them in."

"Sure, no problem."

She scribbled her signature under the 'received line' and as she handed it back to the driver, she caught the sound of music.

A guitar playing.

Singing.

The singing was soft and the bounce from the empty church added an effect that made who was singing and what hard to determine.

Her hand was paused in the middle of returning of the clipboard.

"Haley, are you okay?" he asked,

"Yes. Sorry." She released it. "I wasn't expecting music."

"Sounds good. Love that song. Never heard a guy sing it."

Haley was slightly dumbfounded. The delivery driver had great ears or something, but it took until he walked to the door and Haley closed the office until she heard it.

She inched closer to the church staying in the hall. She had an inkling of who it was, but she had to look. The words were modified, she recognized the song.

I was so scared, he sang, *I threw my hands up in the air ...*

Not wanting to be seen, she peeked in.

Jesus take the wheel ...

Chip.

He stood on the stage where the contemporary band played, acoustic guitar in hand. He stood strumming, moving slightly in a pace, while singing. The teens from the group filed on stage, sitting down to watch.

It took her breath away, stumbling her back into the wall in shock.

I'm letting go, give me one more chance ...

It wasn't the surprise of him playing or singing, somehow, a part of her expected that. But to hear him not only playing and singing with emotions, but him showing those emotions was astonishing.

Keep going, she thought. I want to hear more.

He had to be on autopilot, he was obviously moved to play by some feeling inside of him.

For as much as she was in the moment, she was pulled out of it with the chattering voices of her father and the chief as they entered the hall.

"Haley, guess what the Chief got ..."

"Shh." She hushed him, crinkling her face.

At first her father was confused by her request, then his eyes widened, and he whispered as he pointed with surprise. "Is that Chip?"

"Yes." She nodded. "Listen to him. Look at him."

"Oh ... wow."

Haley's head swayed side by side, eyes closed as she listened.

I know I have to change. From now on tonight ...

As soon as he blasted again into the chorus, her hand went to her heart and the other lifted in praise.

"What a gift," Pastor Rick said. "What a gift he didn't know he had."

"It's unreal. It's what we need and are missing."

"No, Haley," Her father placed his hand on her back. "It's what he needed and was missing. Wow, we are learning something new about him every day." He looked back at Russ. "Don't we, Chief?"

"Yeah." The chief had his phone pulled out and he was looking down to it. "Yeah, we do."

SEVENTEEN

The apartment was a mess, not that Grant expected Jonas' place to be any different. A studio style apartment, one of probably ten that were above a huge collectible store.

Clothes were strewn everywhere, dishes in the sink and on the coffee table. Empty little foil seasoning packets from Ramen noodles were all over the place.

The fact that it had been so long since the garbage had been taken out or the pizza boxes tossed, caused a moldy smell in the place.

Even with all the clutter, it felt empty.

Grant went for his run and ended up there.

Immediately upon entering, he started cleaning up, tossing clothes in a bag so he could launder them. He used a pine cleaner to give it a fresh scent and did the best he could with a broom. Jonas didn't have a vacuum.

He was overwrought with worry and sadness, he needed answers. It had been two weeks since he saw his son, spoke to him or heard from him.

This was different than the last time Jonas disappeared.

When it happened before, Cate went immediately to the police. They told her to wait seventy-two hours. Sure enough, even though they hadn't heard from him, Grant was able to see his phone was used because he was on their plan. Jessie said he was posting on social media and the gas credit card Grant had given him 'just in case' ended up being used as well.

Within a week they heard from him.

He called it a party train, but it was really an eight day bender.

Now Jonas' phone hadn't made a call or sent a text since before his gig. The gas card ... untouched.

Were there even answers to get? Wouldn't they have them already? Grant didn't feel confident the police were giving their all looking for him. They had other things they deemed more important and Grant understood that.

Jonas' laptop was on the coffee table, the battery had long since died and Grant plugged it in. He watched it boot up then entered the password. Grant knew what it was because he gave that laptop to Jonas.

Grant opened up the internet browser. Perhaps looking at his sons' browsing history would give him a clue, then he saw the bank icon under frequently visited.

He hadn't used the gas card, was he spending money with his debit? Grant clicked on the link to the bank. The login information was saved and Grant hit 'sign in'.

Jonas had a low balance of forty-three dollars and the only recent activity was an automatic deduction for a streaming service.

He scrolled down, prior to that was an ATM withdrawal on the day he last saw Jonas and the only other transactions that day was before the withdraw and that was a Money Match transfer from Catherine Truett.

Money Match was a way Cate had sent Jonas money when he needed it through an app. Grant had no idea how often she was transferring money to him. It seemed like every couple days, which also coincided with a trip to the store. Grant was willing to bet it wasn't all for groceries.

He closed the bank site and then hit Jonas' social media. Again, he was able to log in with the saved password.

Jonas' screen name was Jupiter Tee, with a skull and guitar tattoo as a profile picture. There were pictures of Jonas at gigs, at bars drinking with friends. Grant searched for the last time Jonas had posted and it had been weeks. Others had posted on his page.

Dude, where you been?

Get together at Patsy's for Jonas June 30th. A good party may bring him out.

Grant hesitated. His fingers hovering the keyboard, then finally he started to type, and he posted on Jonas' wall.

This is Jonas/Jupiter's dad, Grant Truett. If anyone hears or sees my son, please let the family know. We are deeply concerned and want him safe.

Click – Post.

Without exiting the site or the browser, Grant closed the laptop, sighed out, bringing his hands to his face. He turned when he heard the door open. For a brief second, he thought it was Jonas and his heart skipped a beat.

Cate walked in.

"Hey," Grant said.

"Hey." She closed the door. "You stood me up at Sandy's. I went to church, came home, you weren't there. I thought maybe you went ahead to the restaurant. I was wrong. All these years of going there you've never stood me up."

"I'm sorry. I am. I lost track of time."

"Cleaning, I see." Cate set down her purse and walked over to him, sitting next to him on the couch. "I popped by the other day. Just, you know, to see."

"You didn't say anything."

"No, I didn't."

"How'd you know I was here?" Grant asked.

"A hunch. I remember the last time Jonas went missing, I came here daily. Each time hoping to find him sleeping."

"When he came home, he acted like nothing was wrong."

"I know," Cate said. "I was so relieved to see him, I couldn't get mad. I had it in my mind he was dead. At least you know those first couple days."

"I know that feeling now." Grant rubbed his hands together. "It's been two weeks. Two weeks. He hasn't used the phone or his debit card. People are posting on his social media looking for him. They're having a party next Saturday hoping to draw him out. It's like a memorial and it's killing me." Grant abruptly stood and started to pace. "This whole thing ... is killing me. It's like our kid is missing, but because he's bad news or an addict, he ranks low on the importance scale."

"I don't think that's it. It's just the last time I spoke to the detective they still have no evidence to point to foul play."

"People don't just vanish, Cate."

"Yeah, they do. Always a reason, sometimes it's never known."

"How!?" He raised his voice. "Can you be so calm?"

"Because you're not. And I just can't do this anymore, Grant. I love Jonas, I love him with every ounce of my soul, but I can't do this anymore. What you're feeling, how you're acting has been me. Every day, worse on Saturdays for the last four years. You know, this right now, is out of our control. There's nothing we can do. But wait."

"No." Grant shook his head. "I can't. Something is pulling me, and I just can't. Tuesday is my last day of class before my leave, then I'm packing the truck and taking off."

"I thought you weren't doing that," Cate said. "You haven't said anything in a week."

"Yeah, well, you and I haven't been talking much."

"What are you going to do, Grant? Just ... go out there and look. Look where? How?"

"I'm retracing his steps that night and go from there. I don't care, I'm doing this," Grant said. "I will find our son."

Doctor Jenner sat in his office at the hospital, staring at a sheet of paper, while Russ watched him as if waiting for some specific reaction.

"Why am I looking at a picture of a guitar?" Doctor Jenner asked.

Russ set his mug on the desk.

"Ah." Jenner shifted his eyes from the mug to the picture.

"The patterns are a dead ringer for each other."

"They are."

"Are you thinking of getting this guitar? I thought you hated that mug."

"I do. And I came to ask your opinion. When Chip saw this mug last week, he said the pattern looked very familiar. I was at Guitar World and that guitar was on sale. It was brought into the store to pawn."

"And you think this is Chip's?"

"I don't know. A week ago, I wouldn't have thought twice about it. But the kid's memory is creeping back. He gardens, knows about mixing sound, and plays the guitar really well."

"Did you ask Chip about it?"

Russ shook his head. "I will when I have more of the facts."

"What's the guitar store telling you?" Doctor Jenner asked.

"Not much. The manager confirmed only that it wasn't our Chip that brought it in. He wass being kind of a hard nose. I get it. There are laws regarding pawning. I have to get a court order in that jurisdiction," Russ said. "Shouldn't be hard since we are dealing with a John Doe case. But I won't be able to try until Monday."

"You're really looking into this?"

"I have a hunch this guitar will help his identity. Just a hunch."

"Yes, but if this is his guitar, how does the guitar of a kid from Kansas or Missouri end up in a Nebraskan Guitar World?"

"May he sold it to someone before the accident? I just don't think Chip was as clean cut as he looks to be now."

Doctor Jenner nodded. "Reminds me of the Baker boy."

"Exactly."

"He could have had the guitar on him. I mean middle of the night," Jenner said. "Maybe playing in his band. It could have gotten thrown from the car. Maybe we didn't see it, and someone found it days later."

"Or that night."

"Like one of our EMS workers?" Jenner asked.

"More like ... the passenger."

Jenner leaned back and breathed out heavily.

"What? You don't think that?" Russ asked.

"No, actually, I don't. I don't believe anyone was in that car with him. One, he was given a hallucinogenic and he was heavily under the influence. And two, that crash was brutal. The chances of a second person not only lucky enough to walk away, but walk away and steal a guitar ..." he shook his head. "No. It's near impossible."

Russ took back the picture and folded it. "I feel so strongly this is a lead."

"Then follow it. But I don't think it was a passenger."

"Thanks, Doc." Russ stood. "I'll let you get back to work. I'm headed to the church."

"For your coffee?"

"Think I'll check out services."

Doctor Jenner laughed. "You? Russ, come on. Why the suspicion all of the sudden?"

"It's not suspicion, it's the need to know the truth. You don't think ... you don't think he's faking this all do you?"

"Chip? The amnesia?"

"Yes."

"Why would you think he is?"

"Because that kid picked up a guitar, played and sang a difficult song, without effort, like he played it a hundred times."

"He probably did," Doctor Jenner said.

"How does someone with amnesia not remember their name, yet remembers someone in the car with them, and how to play guitar?"

"Amnesia doesn't work that way," Jenner explained. "The brain is complicated. Amnesia affects memory, right? There are two types of memory. Declarative and procedural. Declarative is something you force yourself to remember, like studying for a test. Procedural is stuff we learn in life and it becomes a habit or something we do without thought. Walking, talking, eating, riding a bike. He may have gardened and played his guitar all his life. That's procedural."

"And you don't think he's faking?" Russ asked.

"I can't believe you do. You can't fake that accident or the brain swelling. If he's faking, he's a heck of an actor. What's the gain, why fake?"

"Maybe he's a criminal or running and hiding. Maybe he wants to gain our trust and get all he can from us and take off."

Doctor Jenner's mouth opened dramatically. "Wow. Once bitten twice shy is an understatement with you. I know you watched it happen. I know you watched good people in this town get misled then ripped off. "

"Yes, I did, and it all seems too familiar," Russ said.

"It's not the case here, Russ. It's not a repeat of the Baker kid."

"When we met him he was angry, confrontational, combative and arrogant. Now he's … look at him. I just … I have a hard time believing someone you know can just move in with a pastor, work at a church and …" Russ snapped his finger. "Flip the personality switch. Can someone with amnesia have a polar opposite of a personality change?"

"Yes. Yes, they can. Especially if they don't remember who they were, they'll adapt to their surroundings."

"And when he remembers who he is?" Russ asked.

Doctor Jenner shrugged. "Who knows. Maybe he'll like who he became."

Russ felt somewhat satisfied with that response. It was his job to be suspicious. He supposed that was part of his personality. He thanked Doctor Jenner, then went on his way.

He was late. Not that he really went into the church farther than the vestibule when he stopped at the mingle for coffee. Seeing how he was in uniform and expecting people might worry he was there on official police business, he took a seat in the back, last row.

Pastor Rick was before the congregation in his contemporary service, relaxed attire. He held the microphone, paced and was animated when he spoke.

Russ felt it was ironic the pastor spoke of 'trust' when Russ was there because he was suspicious.

"It's a hard thing to do," Pastor Rick said. "Hey, I'm guilty of it, we all are. Giving it to God is easier said than done. Here God, here are my troubles ... oh, wait, they aren't getting resolved, let me have it back. It's like having a thousand dollars and you need someone to hold it. It's hard to trust who you give it to. That's why you need to trust. Sometimes we are so into our instincts and what we believe should happen or could happen, it's difficult to envision God knows what will happen when it is totally different than what we thought our path could be. Speaking of paths, I want to bring someone up here today to play and sing a song for you. This young man miraculously survived an accident. His story is pretty remarkable. He's not expecting this, but when I heard him the other day, especially this song, I knew you had to hear it, too. Chip ... let Haley run the board and come on down here."

Russ turned, like everyone else to the back of the church. Chip was in the proverbial spotlight. Slightly reluctant and somewhat bashful, Chip relented and made his way from the sound board.

Russ watched him walk toward the front as his phone vibrated in his pocket. He was on duty and he had to take it.

The caller ID on the phone read 'Correction Facility' and immediately, Russ jumped up and walked from the church to take the call.

He answered it.

"You are receiving a call from an inmate at the Wyandotte County Correctional Facility, this call may be monitored and recorded."

"Hello?" Russ answered, stepping outside the church. "This is Chief McKibben."

"Officer, McKibben, thanks for filling up my calling card," the male voice said. "I've been out of funds for two weeks. Figured I'd call you back."

"And this is?"

"Wow, how many guys' jail cards do you fill up?" he snickered. "This is Harold Whitmore."

"Harold, thank you for calling me back. I met your grandmother."

"How?"

"Same reason a Nebraska police officer is calling you. Your chevy was involved in an accident."

"When?"

"Two weeks ago."

"That wasn't me," Harold said. "I've been in here rolling through the processing system for two weeks. The chevy? The Impala?"

"Yep, that's the one."

"I haven't had that car in a couple months. I ... I owed some dude some money and he took the car as a tradeoff."

"Why didn't you change the plates?" he asked.

"Didn't get to it," Harold said.

"Who did you give it to?" Russ pulled out a little notebook.

"A guy named Teeter."

"Do you know his whole name?"

"No. Just ... Teeter."

"I see. Can you tell me what he looked like?" Russ asked, glancing back at the church.

"Tall. Like maybe six foot. Skinny, shaved head, he has a bunch of tattoos. A lot on his neck."

"Thank you and where ..." Russ heard the line disconnect and he grunted in frustration. He replaced the phone in his pocket. The tattoo, shaved head guy wasn't Chip. Chip could have stolen it and, considering the shady tradeoff of Harold's car, he doubted the theft would have been reported.

The car mystery had to be put to rest, for the moment it was a dead end.

Russ wasn't giving up. He still had the guitar. He was close and he truly felt in his gut the mystery of Chip Doe would be solved sooner than later.

EIGHTEEN

Standing outside the driver's door of Grant's truck, Cate handed him the thin, stainless steel thermos. "Coffee. Don't pour while you're driving."

"I won't."

"And ..." She held up a small cooler. "Snacks for the hotel and the road. There is a sandwich in there."

Grant took them both placing them inside his truck. "Cate, listen, thank you. Thank you for supporting this."

"Why wouldn't I?"

"Because it's crazy."

"No." She shook her head. "No, it's not. I think you need this as much as you need to find Jonas."

"You're right."

"So, what's the plan?" Cate folded her arms.

"I'm going to check into the hotel. The same one Jonas stayed at. He had checked in earlier in the day, we know that. Maybe they moved his room. We've had that happen to us. Then I'm going to the Rat-Tat-Tat to talk to the bartender. Chelsey is her name. She was working that night."

"You called ahead to see when she's working?"

Grant nodded. "I did. She'll be there this afternoon. Then I'll just drive around, hit every town, put up those flyers I made. I have to do something Cate, I just can't sit around and wait."

"I know. I am very proud of you."

Grant leaned into her and kissed her, then embraced Cate. "Thank you. I will call you and give updates."

"Thank you."

Grant stepped back and got in the truck. "I love you."

"I love you, too." She closed the door and moved out of the

way.

Cate stood watching as Grant pulled out of the driveway and onto the road. He extended his arm out the window and waved as he drove off.

She closed her eyes and said a prayer that one way or another, Grant would find what he needed.

It was the most recent picture Grant could find of Jonas and had taken it from his social media. He was holding his guitar, a partial smile on his face. It was hard to find a picture of Jonas smiling because for the last several years he was so unhappy, he rarely smiled.

Grant felt like he had failed. Failed at getting close to Jonas, getting to know him on a different level. He was a staunch believer in being the parent and not the friend, so much so that when Jonas got older, Grant lost his chance to have that closeness, that happy medium between friend and parent.

Jonas gravitated more toward Cate. Although there were times in his adult life she mothered Jonas like he was an eleven year old boy again.

Now, when he looked down at the flyers, the word 'Missing' big and bold above his son's picture, Grant feared he would never get a chance again with his son.

He wasn't a bad father. Rarely raised his voice, provided for his family, was there if his kids needed him. He just didn't know if he did enough, maybe if he had done more.

It was surreal for Grant, hanging that first flyer at the rest stop. He made notes of towns he passed, tiny places he'd go back and check.

He had printed up hundreds of flyers and he'd hang them all. He'd make more if he had to. Someone somewhere had to have seen Jonas or know what happened to him.

Grant arrived at the hotel and checked in. It took him a little longer because he stopped several times on the way. The manager was there, and she took time to talk to him.

The police had spoken to her and she told Grant the same thing she told them. He never checked out and she had even looked on the security cameras.

Jonas had not returned that night.

His belongings were left in the room. An overnight bag, toothbrush, fifth of whiskey and a bag of chips. The hotel had them gathered in one clear plastic bag and it was placed in lost and found.

It felt like a slam to his chest when she handed it to him.

He was on his way to his next search location and took the clear bag out to the truck. His son's things were not garbage. That was the way Grant saw it even though he knew the hotel didn't mean anything by putting his items in a plastic bag. It was their procedure.

Sitting in the driver's seat, Grant removed Jonas' things. The second he touched, smelled the overnight bag, Grant was swept up in a wave of sadness which struck him deep in his soul. Was this it? Was this all he had left of his child?

He placed the bag on the floor by the passenger seat, then grabbed the steering wheel.

He held tight, gripping hard as his forehead rested against the wheel.

It took everything he had not to break down.

Get it together, get it together, he told himself, *you have a plan.*

After a few moments, Grant started the engine. It was time to go to that bar.

Denied.

The county judge denied Russ.

Guitar World wanted a search warrant to give up the surveillance video and information about the individual selling the guitar. Stating they were protecting the rights of the individual. The judge agreed. He saw no reason or connection between that guitar and Chip Doe.

He told Russ, "Exhaust all other means first and I will reconsider."

Russ knew he hadn't exhausted all means, there was still one.

Fingerprints.

If Chip had a record, and Russ was pretty sure he did, then his identity would come up.

He returned from the county courthouse frustrated and planned on talking to Chip.

But first he wanted to talk to Marge and Old Joe.

Russ headed over to Baker's Market. It was the lunch rush, and on a Wednesday which was Marge's Meatball Sub special.

Marge was in the café, not only overseeing the cooking and clerks, but she was hands on. Old Joe sat at a small table, reading a magazine, probably on his third latte. He was done with working, he claimed he was retired but was always at the market.

Like he had a radar on him, Old Joe looked up when Russ walked by and to the counter.

"What's up?" Joe asked. "Getting a meatball special?"

"They do smell awfully good. Maybe when I leave," Russ said. "I just wanted to talk to Marge and you know what, you're here, maybe you can join us?"

"What's going on?"

"I need your opinion on something."

"Good luck pulling her away."

"It won't take long." Russ didn't foresee Marge giving him grief about taking a break for a minute or two.

Then again, Russ never asked her to step away from the floor on Meatball Wednesday.

Marge complied reluctantly. Joe joined Russ and Marge in the little back office and Russ barely got the word, "Fingerprints" out before Marge lit up.

"No," Marge said. "Absolutely not. No."

"Can I ask why?" Russ questioned. "I mean, come on, Marge this is a way to find out who he is."

"By proving he's some sort of criminal?" Marge snipped. "The fingerprints could be a dead end."

"Then I need to try." Russ waved a finger. "I don't need to ask for your permission. He'll do it if I say something to him."

"Then don't say anything. When he got out of the hospital, he said to you and me he was giving himself a time limit. He wanted a month to let his memory come back. Give him that time. What is the big deal, Russ? Huh? Why do you want his memory back?"

"Because he doesn't," Russ said. "If he has amnesia ..."

"If? If?" Marge argued.

"Okay. Bad word choice," Russ defended. "But he doesn't want it back. Want to know why? Because he knows, deep down inside he's trouble and he doesn't want to remember that person."

"And is that so bad?" Marge asked. "Is it so bad he wants to move forward?"

"You can't move forward," Russ said. "Without looking at the truth." Russ heard the soft chuckle come from Old Joe. "What Joe?"

"What's so funny is, he remembered what his passenger said," Joe replied. "And if I'm not mistaken, it was those words. Strange. Eerie. I got chills."

Russ just shook his head. "Just stop with that."

"Hey!" Marge blasted. "Don't you scoff at my husband. You're searching Russ. Are you so bored in this town you have to run to Fremont to dig up something?"

"What are you talking about, Marge?" Russ asked.

"Oh, Doc Jenner told us how you are chasing a guitar in Fremont. Trying to get surveillance footage, find out who sold the guitar to the store."

"Yes." Russ nodded. "I think it's Chip's and I think whoever pawned it might be the passenger."

Old Joe spoke up. "Could you not chase that one?"

"Why?"

"Does it matter?" Joe asked. "I mean, I don't think it has anything to do with you thinking the guitar was stolen. The passenger doesn't matter to you, but he does to Chip. Instead of being stalled, Chip's moving forward, memory or not. He believes he knows who the passenger was. Let it go. Let his belief do the wonders."

"Okay," Russ held out his hand. "You can believe in that stuff, but I don't have to—"

"Stuff?" Marge cut him off. "You stop right there Russ McKibben, one more word scoffing at beliefs and I will ban you from my market, law or not. This is so like you. We should have known."

"What are you talking about?" Russ asked.

"You." Marge waved her hand around. "All good hearted at first. All good intentions. Trying to help, getting the pastor to take him in. Oh, yeah, that's you. For about a week, then your mind goes, and you get suspicious or doubtful. You're doing it again, turning your back, believing the bad and finding the negative, just like you did with our boy."

"He is not your boy!" Russ blasted.

"No! He's not," Marge said emotionally, then calmed. "No. He's not. Because I will not let you, me, or anyone else in this town give up on him. Like we all did ... with my boy." Saying no more, Marge turned and left the office.

They stood in silence, then Joe cleared his throat and stood. He paused by the door. "Did you ever ... ever lose your glasses?"

"Huh?" Russ asked, confused.

"You know, lose your glasses. You look and you look, then suddenly you realize they're on your nose or right there by your coffee. How did you miss them, right? Same can be said about answers, Chief. Sometimes you aren't gonna see the answer if you look too hard, you gotta just ... sit back and let the answers come to you. Have a good day, Chief."

It was a courtesy that Russ went to Marge and Old Joe, he didn't need to. He did so because they, like the pastor, had taken

Chip under their wing. It was a strong wing, and they were protecting him. Perhaps Russ did need to follow Old Joe's advice and step back.

It was something else to think about.

◆ ◆ ◆

The Rat-Tat-Tat Bar and Grill was not what Grant expected, then again, he didn't know what to expect. A large, log cabin looking place with a front porch as wide as the building. It was set off the main roadways so far, Grant wondered how they got any business.

He carried a flyer with him when he walked in. Not that he expected them to hang it up, but he had to try.

The young female bartender was behind the bar looking up to the television as she leaned against a cooler, and one other customer was there. A man sat at the far corner of the bar, eating a burger while looking at his phone.

The bartender noticed him, smiled and walked up to Grant as he approached the bar.

"Hi," she said. "What can I get you?"

"Nothing. Are you Chelsey?"

"I am."

"My name is Grant Truett."

The smile dropped from her face and she drew a look of compassion. "Oh, yeah, my manager told me you would be stopping by. Still no word on your son?"

Grant shook his head and inched the flyer her way.

She lifted it. "Yeah, I remember him. Really talented guy."

"Thank you. You were working that night?"

"I was."

"His drummer said he got into a fight?"

Chelsey nodded. "He did. A scuff, short fight with Lance, one of our regulars."

"Was he hurt maybe? Like something that would have a delayed reaction?"

"Not that I know of. He played the next set. But can you hold on, I have something for you." She lifted her finger then darted from behind the bar to the back room. She wasn't gone long, and when she returned she set the black wallet down in front of Grant.

Grant sighed out a silent aching moan when he saw it. "His wallet. He didn't have his wallet or ID."

"He dropped that in here before he left ... the police didn't tell you?" she asked.

Grant shook his head. "They didn't tell us much about what you told them, just that they didn't suspect any foul play."

"He was fine when he left. I mean ... he looked tired, said he was hungry or something like that," Chelsey said. "I mean I only served him two drinks. One was really early on, the other was at the end of the night when Doug bought him one."

"Who is Doug?"

"Another regular. A friend of Lance, he got him the drink to make up for the fight. But when I left there was only my car and the waitress' truck."

"Was there any way he could have been jumped maybe?"

"I don't know. I mean, the car was ..." her attention was drawn away when another customer, a man entered the bar. "Hold on." She turned from Grant. "Can I get you something?"

"I have a takeout order for Jeff," he said.

"Two orders of wings and a burger?" Chelsey asked.

"That's it."

"Almost done. Can I get you something while you wait?"

"Nah, I'm good." He slid onto a stool.

Chelsey returned her attention to Grant. "I'm sorry I couldn't be more help."

"No, I appreciate it. I do. Can you ..." He began to slide the flyer to her but paused. He glanced at Jeff, the man at the bar. "Sir, hi, are you from this area?"

Jeff looked over. "I'm working in the area. I live about eight miles east of here."

"I'm looking for my son. Can you take a look and see if you saw him around?"

"Sure."

Chelsey took the flyer over to the man.

Jeff stared at it then shook his head. "No, man, I'm sorry. I haven't seen him. Quite a ways from Iowa City."

"He was playing a gig here," Grant replied.

"Sorry. I wish I could help." Jeff returned the flyer to Chelsey.

She took it over to the other customer then returned. "He hasn't seen him. I'll be more than happy to have this behind the bar and show people."

"I would really appreciate that," Grant said.

"And you checked all the hospitals? Jails?" she asked.

"We have exhausted every hospital, jail, even rehab. There were no accidents that night. His name wasn't registered. Or even..." he lifted the wallet. "A John Doe."

"John Doe?" Jeff spoke up with question to his voice. "When was this? When did he disappear?'

"We haven't seen him in two and a half weeks," Grant replied.

"Not sure when it was, but there was a big accident on Broke Man's Curve a little while ago. Week, two weeks, I'm not sure. The guy pretty much walked away with only a little bit of injuries, which..." he fluttered his lips. "Was a miracle. Lots of wrecks there. No one ever survives. He lost his memory though. The local news called him John Doe. Just made me think."

Chelsey snapped her finger. "Oh, that's right. That's the guy they're saying claimed Jesus was in the car with him."

"Um, He had to be in the car with him," Jeff replied. "Just saying."

Grant's head spun. "Wait. There was an accident with a John Doe? We checked every hospital in the state. No one said anything about a John Doe."

"Iowa?" Jeff asked.

"Yes."

"Uh, yeah, that's why," Jeff said. "Broke Man's Curve is in

Nebraska. About twenty-five miles from here. I think they mentioned Williams Peak. Pretty sure it was Williams Peak Hospital."

Grant felt instantly deflated. "Thanks, but that's west, he would have been headed east."

"It's west on eighty instead of east," Jeff said. "It was late. You said he had a gig. It was dark. Could be an easy mistake. You came all this way already, what's another thirty miles to check it out?"

Grant suddenly perked back up. "You're right. You are absolutely right. And you know what? That is the first solid lead I have had to follow. Thank you." He backed away from the bar, stopped, pulled out his wallet and put money on the bar. "Buy this man his lunch and keep the change. Thank you so much. Both of you." He headed to the door.

"Good luck." Jeff lifted his hand.

"Let us know," Chelsey added.

Something stirred in Grant, it was an exhilaration he hadn't felt in weeks. He hurried out of the bar. As soon as he stepped to his truck, he looked at the road and it took him a second to remember which way he came in. Grant smiled. If he couldn't tell in the middle of the day, surely Jonas could have been confused on direction at night.

The moment he got into the truck, before he drove off, he picked up his phone to call Cate and let her know about the hopeful news.

Williams Peak was about as picturesque as any small town depicted in the movies. Grant was amazed at how clean it was. The buildings and stores were all in great condition. Tree lined sidewalks with outdoor cafes.

He thought about showing the flyer, but instead opted to go to the police station. If there was an accident and a John Doe, surely, they would know about it.

After getting directions from a very nice man at the gas station, Grant found the station and pulled in a spot by the road across the street.

He paused before crossing, but traffic stopped to let him go. He had never seen anything like it.

A female officer was seated at a desk by the door when he walked in.

Grant approached her. "Hi, Ma'am, would there be someone in charge I could speak to?"

She glanced up to him, but as her mouth opened to reply, a taller man stepped closer.

"That would be me," he said walking to Grant. "I'm Chief McKibben, how can I help you?'

Grant was nervous, his stomach twitched, and hand shook a little. "I'm Grant Truett."

"How can I help you, Mr. Truett?"

"I may be way off. Like three hundred miles off. But I heard there was an accident and ... and my son is missing. I'm looking for my son." Grant held up the flyer. "Have you seen him?"

Chief McKibben looked down to the flyer and lifted it. "Come into my office."

NINETEEN

Losing a child is every parent's worst nightmare, Russ knew this. As a father himself, he hated that he had left Grant hanging, sitting alone in his office with no answers. But there was more to it than just saying, 'Yes, we know where your son is.'

Russ wasn't a medical expert, not by a long shot. Even he was aware there had to be cautionary steps taken with amnesia victims.

He called in reinforcements for the talk with Grant Truett.

"Marge can you and Old Joe come to the station," Russ called them at the store. "It's important. Nothing bad. Please, I'll explain when you get here."

"On their way?" Doc Jenner asked.

"Yes. Should only be a minute."

Jenner leaned back and glanced into Russ' office; he lowered his voice. "Did you say anything to him?"

Russ shook his head. "I thought it would be best if we all explained, and you tell us how to handle this."

It wouldn't take long for Marge and Joe to show up. Russ knew that. They were only a block away.

They, like Jenner, arrived within five minutes. Mr. Truett had been kept waiting a little over ten minutes, which to him must have seemed like a lifetime.

Marge and Joe had no clue what was going on when they showed up, and it was written all over their faces.

Just outside his office. Russ stopped them. "There's someone here you need to meet. He's in my office."

Marge and Joe walked in ahead of Jenner and Russ.

Grant turned around in his seat, standing when the group

entered.

"You're him," Joe said. "You're his father."

Russ looked quickly at Joe. "How did you know that?"

"I just did. This is fantastic." Joe extended his hand to Grant.

Marge just stepped forward and embraced him. "Oh, you poor man, I know what you have been going through."

Grant trembled. "Please don't tell me my son has passed."

Gasping, Marge stepped back. "No, no. I'm sorry you took it that way."

"Are you guys like a town council?" Grant asked. "What … what has my son done? He's done something bad, hasn't he?"

"Have a seat." Russ indicated to the chair. "This is not a town council. More of a council of your son."

"I don't understand. Is he okay?"

Russ nodded. "He is. This is Doctor Jenner. He treated your son. And these two are Marge and Joe Baker, they treated your son with absolute kindness and were the ones who saved his life that night on the road."

"He was the one in the accident?"

Russ nodded.

Grant glanced at Marge and Joe. "I can't begin to thank you enough, all of you."

Doctor Jenner leaned against the Chief's desk. "While he only suffered minor bodily injuries, he did have a head injury and some swelling. Physically, he's better. But he has memory loss."

"Amnesia?" Grant asked.

"Yes. It's coming back. Are you familiar with the term procedural memory?" Jenner questioned.

"I am. That's like riding a bike."

"Exactly. Things like that are coming fast for him. For example, the guitar," Jenner said. "According to the Chief, he just picked it up and played it like a pro, not knowing why."

"That doesn't surprise me," Grant said. "The guitar has been an extension of his body since he was twelve. It also wouldn't surprise me if you told me he was gardening."

Everyone looked at each other.

"He is," Russ said. "Nice work, too."

"Well, he gets that knack from his mom," Grant replied. "He worked landscaping in the summer. Has he started baking yet?"

"Baking?" Marge asked with shock. "Chip bakes?"

"Chip?" Grant asked. "You call him Chip?"

Marge nodded. "We all do. That's me, I called him Chip because I figured he has to be a chip off the block of someone. So, he bakes."

"He makes amazing cookies."

"What is his name?" Old Joe asked.

"Jonas. His name is Jonas," Grant replied. "I … I don't understand. Why not run his prints?"

"I wanted to," said the Chief. "Would we have matched them?"

"Oh, yeah, Jonas has not been on a good path for the past few years. DUI, public drunkenness, a couple disorderly conducts," Grant said. "Why didn't you run them if you wanted to?"

Marge answered, "Chip wanted to wait until he got his memory back before he found out who he was. He wanted to remember instead of being told."

Doc Jenner spoke up, "It's not that we didn't try to find out who he was. The fingerprints were going to be the last resort at the one month mark. The VIN on the car was a bust."

Grant nodded. "He borrowed it from a guy named Teeter, and I don't even want to know where he got it from. Teeter's a dealer and in jail right now. You wouldn't have had any idea who he was." Grant sank back in the chair. "He dropped his wallet at the bar where he played his show. And I will need to go back there to thank the man who suggested I come here."

"Have you been there?" Russ asked.

"I was just there," Grant answered. "The state police weren't giving me any answers. As a father I just needed to ask my questions. He wasn't drunk, at least that's what the bartender said. She told me he had two drinks. One earlier in the night and someone named Doug bought him one at the end."

"Is this Doug a friend?" Russ asked.

Grant shook his head. "No. According to the bartender he was a friend of the guy Jonas fought with that night. Was buying him a drink, I guess to make amends."

Hurriedly, Russ pulled out his tablet. "You said the guy's name was Doug?" He wrote it down. "Would this bartender know how to find him?"

Grant stammered. "I guess. I think she said he was a regular."

"Where is this bar?" questioned Russ.

"Outside of Persia, Iowa."

Russ looked at Doctor Jenner. "Have your son call up the Iowa state police. I wonder if we can get this guy to admit it."

"I don't understand," Grant said. "What's going on?"

Doctor Jenner turned to Grant. "That last drink your son had … was spiked. Someone put a date rape or club drug into it."

"Someone deliberately did this to my child?" Grant asked with emotions. "They had to know he was driving. They had to know." He brought his hand to his face.

Marge rested her hand on Grant's shoulder. "The Good Lord was watching out for him."

"In fact," Joe added. "He was riding in the car with him."

Slowly, Grant lowered his hand. "Is my son saying Jesus was in the car with him?"

"Spoke and saw him." Joe replied.

"Okay. Okay." Russ stopped them. "We can discuss that later. And no, Marge, I'm not scoffing at your husband. I have a question to ask." He walked over to his desk, opened the drawer and pulled out a piece of paper.

Marge, Old Joe and Jenner all groaned.

"For goodness sakes," Jenner said. "Let that go."

"I can't. I have to know." He handed the paper to Grant. "Do you recognize this?"

"Yep, it's my son's guitar. He had it custom made," Grant answered.

"Ha!" Russ gloated. "I knew it. Call it a hunch. I knew this was his and it's stolen property."

Grant shifted his eyes around to everyone. "Could this have something to do with the spiked drink?"

"We can find out." Russ put the picture down. "For now, we need to take you to Chip."

Doc Jenner interjected. "We need to not overwhelm him. Maybe Grant, Marge and Joe go over. We don't know if he'll remember right away when he sees his father. He may, he may not. He also may have some physical repercussions if it hits him too fast. Anything is possible."

"And if he doesn't remember his father?" Joe asked.

"Doesn't mean he won't in an hour or a few days," Doc Jenner answered. "After steady exposure. I think for the first introduction, if Chip doesn't remember his father, we don't say anything. It might be too much; he may not trust it. Are you prepared for that reaction?" he asked Grant. "It might be painful he doesn't know you."

Grant nodded. "I can handle it. I can handle anything because he is alive."

"Good." Marge extended her hand. "Let's go see your son. Did you want to call your wife first?"

"No." Grant shook his head. "Not until I see him with my own eyes. Then when I do, I'll let her know the good news."

"As a mother myself I can tell you," Marge said. "It will be the best news of her life."

Haley was hesitant at first. She took a bite under pressure, chewed apprehensively for a second, then she stopped. Her eyes widened. "Oh, my goodness, Chip." She brought her fingers to her mouth to catch the crumbs and she chuckled. "These are amazing."

"You think?"

"Yes!" She took another bite, closed her eyes and leaned against the wall in the back hall as she enjoyed her treat. "They melt in your mouth."

"They're just butter cookies, that's all your dad had the ingredients for. He doesn't really make anything from scratch."

"No." Haley smiled. "No, he doesn't. You aren't gonna happen to discover you sew, are you?

Jonas laughed. "I don't think so. But who knows. Wait, you have …" he reached her chin, and using his thumb he brushed away crumbs.

Haley paused, looking at him as he did so. "Thank you."

There was a moment there, just a brief moment of quiet.

Haley cleared her throat. "So, did you find a recipe for these?" She finished the cookie.

"No, I didn't. It just came to me."

"Wow. That is crazy how the mind works. I think someone totally domesticated you and you …" she stopped.

"And I what?" Jonas asked.

"Chip," her voice dropped. "What if you're married?. I didn't even think about that"

"I don't think I am. I don't feel like I am." He lifted his left hand. "Wouldn't I wear a ring?"

"You may not. But … okay, we need to get back to the kids. They are waiting for us to take them outside." She reached over and secured the lid on the tin of cookies. "They will enjoy these."

"They are going to tease me. They're teenagers."

"It's a chance you have to take."

"Oh. Wait. I forgot the game pieces. Here." He handed her the tin. "I'll be right there."

"Don't take long."

"They're right in the office."

Tin of cookies cradled in her arms like a baby, Haley stepped into the church.

Grant stopped walking on the pathway. "A church? My son is

in a church? I thought maybe a hospital or institution with the amnesia."

Marge shook her head. "No one wanted him to go to an institution. Not when he was still learning about himself." She and Joe led him to the doors.

It baffled Grant, it truly was the last place he expected to be taken.

When they opened the doors, he heard laughter and a woman's voice saying something.

He was so nervous, his heart beat so strongly, everything sounded muffled and felt dreamlike.

It was a beautiful church. Old fashioned with old style pews on both sides. The walls were a pale blue. They attempted to modernize; Grant could see that.

There was a large altar with a choir section in the back. A stage was built on the left side with steps that led down behind the pulpit.

A group of teenagers were on the stage, a young woman with them.

She walked down the steps to the altar and the teens followed her.

Marge whispered in Grant's ear as they neared. "That's Haley, Pastor Rick's daughter."

When Haley reached the bottom step, she looked over and smiled. "Hey, Maw-Maw, Joe." She turned to the group of teens and instructed them to hang tight, then made her way to the aisle. Her hand extended to Grant. "How do you do, I'm Haley."

"Grant. Grant Truett. Nice to meet you."

"Are you new in town?" Haley asked.

Old Joe answered. "He's in town for a spell. Not sure how long."

"He wanted to see the church," Marge said. "Is Chip around?"

"Oh, he just ran to the office. We're taking the teens outside for group today. He came up with a game. You know how kids like to compete." She crinkled her nose. "He promised he'd play for them after the game. Look." She snickered and held up the tin. "He made cookies."

Marge immediately looked at Grant and placed both her hands around his.

Grant conveyed an 'I told you so' look and then all expression dropped from his face. He felt the blood form a ball and shoot straight to his gut when he saw Jonas step on to the stage.

"Okay, I'm back," Jonas announced. "We can go outside, let me grab a guitar."

"Chip," Haley called him. "Can you come here?"

Grant couldn't blink, he couldn't move. Every bit of his insides trembled, and his mind repeated over and over, 'Look at me. See me. Know me. Please.'

Jonas trotted down from the stage and across the altar to join them.

"Chip, this is Grant Truett," Haley introduced him.

"Nice to meet you, Sir." Jonas extended his hand.

Grant felt like he was frozen in a surreal moment, stuck somewhere in a dream, shaking his son's hand in what seemed like slow motion. Looking into his eyes.

His stomach flipped a little with the slight disappointment Jonas didn't know him. But it was brief, because he was astonished when he looked at Jonas.

Was he the same guy? What happened to him?

He had a couple scars on his face, tiny ones, but his face was fuller and had color. No longer was his hair long, it was short and looked clean. The biggest thing of all … was the way Jonas smiled. He smiled widely and genuinely.

"Nice … nice to meet you, too." Grant felt Marge squeeze his hand for support and he also felt Joe put a hand on his shoulder.

"Mr. Truett is in town for a spell," Haley said. "He's not sure for how long. He wanted to see the church."

"Cool," Jonas said. "Everyone finds a home here. Trust me. We have a really cool, new contemporary service, you should stop by."

"Jonas is now heading up the service as music leader," Haley said. "Millie is so happy about that. Takes the pressure from her."

"Really?" Grant asked. "You pick out the music for services?"

"And play," Jonas replied. "Say, by some chance you don't play, do you?"

"I … I actually do," Grant replied. "I play keyboards, piano."

Jonas looked at Haley then back to Grant. "We are in desperate need of a keyboard player. You wouldn't by chance want to join us while you're in town, would you?"

His request took Grant's breath away and he could barely respond above a whisper, "Son, I would love nothing more than to play music with you. It would mean a lot."

"Awesome." Jonas shook his hand again. "This is great. We have rehearsal tonight at seven."

"I'll be there."

"We'll be waiting. Right now, we have to take the youth group outside." He pointed. "Maw-Maw, Joe, catch you later?"

"You bet, bye, Chip," Marge said, giving another squeeze to Grant's hand and released it.

Grant stood, unable to move. He watched Jonas and Haley gathered the teens. Again, the blood rushed into his ears, muffling the sound of everything but his own fast beating heart.

His arm weighed a ton, and he could barely lift it to wave as the two of them and the teen group left.

"Grant," Marge called him softly. "Are you all right?"

Grant nodded, took a step forward and turned. "My son," his voice cracked, then, trembling with emotions. "I have not … I have not seen him so healthy in …" He closed his eyes. "I haven't seen him smile in …" He choked on his words. "Years. This was more than I expected. This is …" Grant couldn't finish his sentence.

He held it in when he saw his son and everything he fought not to show came barreling forth and Grant was overcome. Weakened by it all, overwhelmed with relief, gratefulness and emotions, in the center aisle of the church, not far from the altar, Grant dropped to his knees and broke down.

TWENTY

Pastor Rick adamantly argued over how unethical he believed it was, he verbally expressed how appalled he was at the notion they weren't going to tell Chip his true identity.

"Do you hear yourselves?" he asked, passionately. "Do you? This young man has been struggling with his identity for weeks and now we know who he is, and you don't think we should tell him? Do you not think this man ..." He pointed to Grant. "Would like nothing more than to tell his son how much he loves him and how worried about him, he was."

Marge shook her head. "You aren't listening. It's not what Chip wants."

"I find that hard to believe." Pastor Rick leaned back in his chair.

"He said it," Marge defended. "The only reason Grant is agreeing to this is because it's his sons wishes."

"I know he said it," Pastor Rick replied. "But did he mean it? Maybe ... just hear me out. Maybe he just knew deep down in his soul he wasn't leading a ... how can I put it, model life? Maybe he knew and just didn't want to have to face it."

"Oh, he did," Marge said. "He told me he didn't believe he was all that well behaved. I'm paraphrasing it nicely. But he didn't want to have that confirmed, he wanted to remember because to quote him, he didn't want himself to have to fit the narrative."

Grant sighed out loudly. "I hope not. To be honest with you Pastor, I'm afraid if we tell him what he was like before, how he acted, either he won't believe it or will feel like everything he is doing here isn't worth it. I'm actually afraid of when he does get his memory back. I don't know how the Chip you know will react to remembering how Jonas was."

"Not telling him because we're afraid doesn't make it any less wrong," Pastor Rick said. "We're just supposed to keep calling him Chip?. Deceiving him? How is he going to feel when he finds out we all knew?"

Old Joe spoke up, "Like we kept our word to his wishes. Besides, how do we know this isn't what God wants?"

"We can't presume to know what God wants," Pastor Rick argued. "Besides, why in the world would God want him to not remember?"

"Oh, that's easy," Marge replied. "Maybe God needs him to see who he can be before he remembers who he was. And maybe God needs you, Grant, to spend time with him and remember who he was before he went down that destructive path. I know these past few years you probably missed him even when he was in the next room. Because he was not the boy you raised, loved or sacrificed for. I know. I bet Chip isn't all that far off from Jonas before troubled times."

Joe added. "But Jonas won't remember even when his memory comes back. When they take a bad path, they pretend that person never existed. It makes them feel better or less guilty about how they are acting."

"As good of arguments as all of you give," Pastor Rick said. "I'm not convinced.'

Marge nodded. "Then let's ask someone else who spends a lot of time with him."

"Who?"

A single knock on the door, then Haley opened it and walked in.

"Wow," Joe said. "The Lord works fast."

Haley looked confused when she entered the office. "I can come back."

"No," Pastor Rick said. "Just the person we needed to see. Come on in. Where is Chip?"

"He's with the group out back. What's going on?" she asked.

"Haley, this is Grant Truett," Pastor Rick said.

Haley nodded. "Yes, we've been introduced."

"But you weren't introduced to him as Chip's father. He's been searching for his son."

"His ... his ..." Haley stuttered. "His father. Mr. Truett, I am relieved to hear you were looking for him. I'm so happy for him. Is his mother here?"

Grant shook his head. "No. She's home. This journey was mine and I have to tell you, I can't believe what I am seeing in my son."

"He's gone through a metamorphosis since the accident," Haley explained. "He was angry and not very nice."

"Yes, well, that sounds like Jonas."

"Jonas." Haley smiled. "That's his name? It's so fitting. I think he may not have remembered who he was, but he held on to how he always felt. Then that faded because he didn't know why he was so angry."

"Haley," Pastor Rick drew her attention. "You don't seem shocked Grant didn't immediately tell Chip who he was."

Haley shook her head. "He was with Maw-Maw, and she knows Chip doesn't want to be told who he is, he wants to remember himself."

"Do you agree with the decision not to tell him yet?" Pastor Rick asked.

"Absolutely." She nodded. "Mr. Truett, I don't know who Chip was before that accident, but I'm sure he is nothing like the Chip we have now. That's because he is free from the burdens that bound him to that personality. He needs to know who he is eventually, yes. But he needs to remember who he is. That's what he wants. For one month, he wants to try to remember and I think we need to give that to him."

"Then it's settled," Pastor Rick said. "We hold off. It's going to be difficult for me, but I will do it."

"In the meantime." Marge grabbed Grant's hand. "This time you will spend with him, talking, playing music. It will be a joy for you getting to spend time with him, seeing him healthy, without the 'walking on eggshell' feeling or worry he will erupt at any time."

"How do you know this so well?" Grant asked.

"Joe and I have been there. Only you have a happier ending," Marge said. "And since I have been there, I need you to resist thinking once he knows who he is, he'll just relapse or this is just another cycle he goes through. It's not, I believe with all my heart it is not."

"You say that with such certainty," Grant said.

"I do and I can. He has a chance to see and experience life through fresh eyes without any preconceived notions or prejudice," Marge explained. "And that … is a gift."

"Are you convinced?" Doc Jenner placed a coffee down in front of Russ as he joined him at a table outside Roasters Café.

"Convinced of what?" Russ asked. "Thank you."

"That's he's not faking it."

"I never said he was."

"Yes, you did."

"No, I suggested it and …" Russ picked up his coffee. "I believe it's real. Old Joe told me he watched Chip. Watched him for signs and Chip didn't even flinch when he saw his father. Not one iota. And Joe knows how someone like Chip can manipulate."

"What now?"

"I think it's wrong not to tell him who he is, but it's the collective decision to hold off for the one month mark, which is in another two weeks. I can hold off."

"I talked to my son," Doc Jenner said. "He'll be calling you. He's going to talk to the state police. But there's very little we can do unless he admits it."

"I don't know about that."

"What do you mean?"

"If we can connect him to that guitar …"

"Russ ..."

"Hear me out. I've been thinking about this since Grant Truett arrived."

"Go on," Doc Jenner said.

"Now ... we know Chip's last drink of the night was drugged. More than likely this Doug guy was the one who did this. A bit of revenge for fighting with his buddy."

Doc Jenner nodded. "Sounds like a motive."

"This guy Doug knows what kind of drug this is and follows Chip. He follows him. Sees him get into the wreck. Now, Chip has told Joe, Marge, you, everyone about this passenger who spoke wisdom, he said, 'I got you' and pulled him out of the wreckage."

"Yes, he did. But what does the passenger have to do with Doug?"

"Doug was following him. You said yourself this drug was hallucinogenic. What if there really wasn't a passenger? What if the guy he thought was in the car was a hallucination of this Doug? The words of wisdom, his own thoughts and remorse. Doug, seeing the crash, pulled him from the wreckage, saw the guitar and took it."

"Why take it all the way to Fremont?"

"Chip went missing in Iowa. Why not another state? Is it far-fetched?"

"The only thing far-fetched is making Doug the passenger," Doc Jenner said. "Everything else, Doug following him, pulling Chip out, taking the guitar, it all fits. Now, all you have to do is prove it."

"Oh, I will. Nothing ever happens in this town. Trust me ..." Russ lifted his coffee. "I'm on it."

Where was Cate?

It had been hours since Grant left the Rat-Tat-Tat and told her he was on his way to Williams Peak to follow a lead. He sent her a text when he arrived at the police station and called her immediately after they left the pastor's office.

No answer.

At first, he thought she was mad at him for not calling right away. But that wasn't Cate's style. He didn't leave a message, he just waited a few minutes and called her again.

After his third call, Grant realized she probably went into work and they weren't allowed to have their phones on the floor. Hating to do so, he sent her a text,

Cate, call me. I found Jonas. He's fine. No, he's better than fine. He's fantastic.

This was not the way to deliver the news, but he didn't want to not let her know.

He went back to the hotel by the bar and checked out. Boasting to the manager he found his son, before returning to Williams Peak, he called the bar and told Chelsey and he thanked her.

Grant decided he was going to stay in Williams Peak. They had a Motel Six just on the outskirts and he got a room there. Jonas had given himself a month's time limit to get his memory back, and since Grant had taken a leave of absence, he had all intentions of staying right there.

He was hoping Cate could take time off as well. They could be there together. Grant was happy, he felt so happy and just wanted to share it with the world, especially Cate.

Once he checked into the Motel Six, he saw it was after four and she would be done working. Still, no answer.

At that point it had been long enough, and Grant started to panic. Had something happened to her? Then he realized she probably just got in the car and was on her way. The moment she heard about a lead; he could see his wife just driving to meet him.

Cate never spoke on the phone in the car. She was one of those people who kept her phone far away.

Figuring that had to be it, he called Jessie.

"Hey, Daddy," she answered the phone.

"Hey, Sweetie. I've been trying to reach your mother. Not sure if you talked to her. I sent her a text. I found Jonas."

Silence.

"Jess."

"Daddy, you found him?" Jessie asked with a shock sound to her voice.

"I did. He's fine, Jessie, he's really fine. He had lost his wallet at the bar and the accident caused some memory loss."

"When ... when did you tell Mom?" Jessie asked.

"A few hours ago."

Suddenly Jessie's voice turned cold. "She didn't say a word to me about you finding my brother."

"You've talked to her."

"Yes."

"Do you know if she's on her way here?" Grant asked.

"No, she isn't on her way there. She's right here."

"With you."

"Yep. Here."

There were a few seconds of quiet.

Cate spoke timidly. "Hello."

"Cate? Cate, where have you been?" Grant asked. "I've been calling and calling."

"I know. I was working. I ... didn't have my phone. I needed to take my mind off of your being out there. I was so nervous. I didn't expect you to get an answer so fast. Then I saw your text."

"If you saw my text why didn't you call me back? You should see him. Oh, Cate, you should see him," Grant gushed. "He's gained twenty pounds. Maybe not that much, but he gained weight. His face is round, his hair is short. He has color and Cate ... he's smiling. He is smiling big time. I couldn't believe it."

Cate didn't reply.

"Why aren't you saying anything?"

"I'm in shock. I mean it's been two and a half weeks. Why didn't he call us? Was he in trouble? Rehab?"

"He was in that accident."

"Still, why didn't he contact us? Does he have any idea how

worried we were?'

"Cate, what is wrong?"

"Does he!" Cate yelled.

"Cate, he has amnesia."

"Really."

"What?"

"Really. And you believe that?" Cate asked.

Grant was thrown through a loop, stunned by her reaction. "Yes. He had a head injury."

"Grant, come on. Amnesia?'

"The doctors ..."

"There is no way to prove or disprove amnesia," Cate said. "You know this. And you also know our son. He hid out, he played this card."

"No. You're wrong. He doesn't know. He really doesn't. He is in this small town and he's changed. Why would you even doubt this?"

"Because I know our son."

"I do, too."

"No," Cate argued. "You don't. Not like I do."

"He's not that good of an actor."

Cate laughed. "You know he is. How many times did he play us? How many times did he break our hearts, my heart for his benefit? This is another one of his games. He's playing whoever he is with and in another week, he is going to walk away from there with everything he can grab."

"Cate, if you would see him, you would know. Come out here. Get in the car ..."

"No."

"Cate."

"No," Cate said. "My heart has been crushed into a million pieces Grant. I have watched him destroy his life and everyone around him. I have grieved for the son he used to be. I have feared for him, prayed for him, enabled him. Now suddenly he is well and healthy in some small town? Wait. He has amnesia. He did it to us again."

"No, Cate, you're wrong. This is me talking," Grant said. "What I am witnessing is nothing short of a miracle."

"Grant, it's nothing short of a con."

"How ... dare you."

"What?" Cate asked shocked.

"How dare you? We have been married for thirty-five years. Been together for forty. In all that time, every single day, every year you have been trying to get me to have faith. To see there is a higher power out there working for our greater good. Finally, after all this time, I witness it. I believe. And what do you do? In so many words, you tell me I'm a fool."

"Grant, that's not what I'm doing," Cate defended.

"Yes, Cate, it is. And do you know what? I don't care, because I am still going to believe. I would love for you to be here, to see this. If not. That's fine. I'm going nowhere. I will be here in this town, with our son, loving and seeing firsthand what a higher power can truly do to change lives."

And with that, not wanting to lose the joy he was feeling over finding Jonas, Grant ended his call with Cate.

TWENTY-ONE

A simple trip to the bath, kitchen and bed store followed by an early dinner. That was the plan Jessie had with her mother. She had spoken to her twice on the phone, several text messages, and not once did she tell her Jonas was found.

It angered Jessie … a lot, but she was cautious about saying anything because she had never seen her mother behave quite like she was at that moment.

Her mother often would be a seesaw of emotions when it came to Jonas, and no doubt he was causing it again. Jessie didn't understand the bitter, angry mood Cate portrayed. After weeks of worrying, hitting brick walls, he was found, and not only was he alive, he was well. Yet, Cate seemed mad about it.

The last time Jonas disappeared he had gone on a binge and the only reason they found him was because Jonas was calling out for his mother in some sort of drug and alcohol induced episode.

A hot mess, barely able to stand, and Cate wasn't mad, she was relieved. Why was her mother acting differently now? Was she in some sort of denial?

Jessie watched her mother hang up and extend it back to her. She knew her father had hung up abruptly. That was evident by the lack of a goodbye and the slight shocked expression on her mother's face.

Her parents were in a fight mode, which was par for course when a difference of opinion rose up over Jonas.

"What's going on with you?" Jessie asked.

"What do you mean?"

"Mom, you didn't tell me about Jonas."

"I know."

"Why?"

"Because a part of me didn't believe it," Cate said.

"You didn't believe he was fine or found?"

"Yes, because to me there was no way he was found alive and fine. They just don't go together, not with your brother. Let's go check out bedding." Cate turned and started walking.

"Mom. Seriously?"

"Jess, I don't want to talk about this with you. Weren't you the one like Jan Brady always saying, Jonas, Jonas, Jonas?"

"That's not right or fair. Actually, that's mean," Jessie said.

"You hated when I talked about him."

"Because you talked about him constantly. We couldn't have a conversation without bringing him. Telling me what he did or didn't do, how bad or good. Have I talked to him?"

"That's why I am not talking about him now."

"It's a little different."

"No, Jess, it isn't," Cate argued. "Talking about Jonas is talking about Jonas, it doesn't matter what the pretext is. You have to be tired of hearing about him."

"You don't get it. It's not because I felt slighted or jealous. It's not because I don't love my brother. I do. It's because I love you and the obsession and worry wasn't good for you."

"I get that. Worry is done. Jonas is fine."

Jessie shook her head when her mother lifted a pillow nonchalantly and looked at the washing instructions. "Jonas isn't exactly fine. He was in a car accident. He has amnesia."

Cate scoffed in the form of a soft laugh.

"You don't believe he has amnesia?"

"No, I don't."

"But Dad said."

"Your father doesn't know Jonas like I do. He's playing these people."

"How can you make that call without even seeing him?" Jessie answered.

"Because I know my son. I know how he uses people to get

what he wants. He messed up somewhere and found a perfect place to hide out. I can't run there, Jessie, I can't go and look in his eyes, hear that manipulative talking. I can't."

"Mom, this isn't about you."

"That's where you're wrong," Cate said. "When dealing with an addict, at some point as a mother, it has to be about me." She turned. "I'm headed to pots and pans."

Then without missing a beat, as if nothing was different or hadn't changed, her mother went to window shop housewares.

Jessie knew her brother probably better than her mother thought and like her mom, she just couldn't accept the amnesia. She couldn't dismiss it either. Jessie would know the truth the moment she looked into Jonas' eyes. For her own sake and her mother's, that was what she had to do.

Marge knew what she was doing, she didn't worry. Her goal was to expose Chip or rather, Jonas, to his father in hopes to stir the memories. She spoke to everyone ahead of time. Don't ask any questions that would force Grant to lie.

She invited Grant to have dinner with them before rehearsal, along with Pastor Rick, Haley and Chip. Even though she knew his real name, he'd always be Chip to her.

Pastor Rick was excited about it, especially when he learned what Marge's plan was. He grabbed an extra rotisserie chicken from Costco.

Marge whipped up some of her sausage, potato stuffing, made a vegetable and grabbed a cake from the market.

Wednesday dinner wasn't usually a big deal.

It was this night.

She hoped maybe some part of Chip would remember his father, but Marge didn't see a spark at all.

"I'm really excited to hear you play," Jonas said at the dinner table. "We didn't talk much, have you been playing long?"

"All my life. I sing some. I'm good on harmonies," Grant replied.

"Awesome, I picked out some cool music. The others already have the charts, but we'll listen before practice. This is my first service as music leader," Jonas told him.

"Not worship leader?" Grant asked.

"Not yet."

"Chip here," Pastor Rick said. "Is new in town as well. Is your family with you?"

"No." Grant shook his head. "My wife is home."

"Any children? Grandchildren?" Marge asked.

"I have two kids. A daughter and son. My daughter is married, my son is not. No grandkids yet." Grant smiled. "I'm hoping."

Jonas asked. "What brought you to Williams Peak?"

There it was, Marge thought, the question she didn't want asked. One that could force Grant to not be honest. But he had that covered.

"I was searching, you know," Grant replied. "I'm a teacher, I needed a break, decided to just hit the road. You get older, there are things you want to do or see. I stopped here. It's great little town. You're new, Chip, what brought you to Williams Peak?"

"A bad night," Jonas said. "I was in an accident. Maw-Maw and Joe found me on the road. I don't know what happened, how it happened or even how I got to the road."

Joe interjected. "I think you do." He shifted his eyes to Grant. "When Chip was in the accident there was a man in the car with him."

"What happened to him?" Grant asked.

"No one knows," Joe replied. "He wasn't there. No sign of him. A lot of us feel it was a higher power at work that night."

Haley added. "Whatever the case, it brought him here, to us," she said. "And I believe this is where he is supposed to be."

Marge watched Grant for a reaction. It was fulfilling and moving to see his expression, such peace on his face. Different than hours earlier when she met him.

She understood. She wished her own son would have transformed in this way. That wasn't in the plan. At least now, she felt in some small way, she had helped Chip, and hoped and prayed with everything in her, unlike her son, Chip would keep going forward.

◆ ◆ ◆

Grant had been in that position before. Looking at his son and seeing a stranger. Listening to him talk and unable to believe it was him speaking. A change of face, body, hair and clothes. He had been there before in Jonas' darkest days. Watching his son whittle away to nothing, barely any meat on his bones, his skin color deathly gray, an unkept man who didn't notice how he looked or even cared, with an attitude so poor and shocking Grant couldn't find any good.

Now here he was the polar opposite.

He couldn't believe he was looking at the same man who argued with him in the driveway nearly three weeks earlier. Even in Jonas' younger days, when he was naïve and untouched by the dark world of addiction, he couldn't recall seeing him look so healthy or with weight.

It was as if someone fed him a constant flow of high caloric food steadily for weeks. Then again, it had only been half a day and already Grant had seen Jonas twice with a milkshake in his hand.

There was actually a milkshake shop in town. Haley said Jonas had been on a milkshake kick for a week, never repeating the same flavor twice and vowing to get through them all.

Whatever it was that was inspiring him to do so, Grant was grateful and loved it.

Grant also loved rehearsal. He watched Jonas play and sing. He always loved listening to him play, but when Jonas went into a strange rock and screaming style of music it was difficult for Grant.

The entire rehearsal Grant was swept up, amazed at Jonas.

He wished he could record or bottle up the joy he felt and save it for a day when he needed it. Grant didn't want the night to end.

But it did.

"Okay is everyone good with that last song?" Jonas asked. "We'll do a reprise at the end after service. It's a good one, hard, but I think everyone will feel it. Are we good?"

Everyone nodded.

"Mr. Truett, that song is new to all of us," Jonas said. "I'm good with rehearsing Friday evening if you want."

"I think that's a good idea," Grant replied. Even though he wasn't familiar with the song before that night either, he was comfortable playing it. He just wanted to hang out with Jonas again.

Any excuse would do.

He helped Jonas pack up, he really didn't have anything else to do before he went back to the hotel.

"Can I ask you something?" Grant said as he and Jonas left the church.

"Sure."

"How do you feel about not remembering who you are? Is it frustrating?"

"It was at first, now I feel like I'll know soon," Jonas replied. "I mean I get these things I call memory feelings."

"What are they?'

"It's a feeling like I know something, I just don't remember why. Like cookie baking and playing music. I also get memory feelings when something isn't right, like when they thought my name was Harold."

"Harold? Grant laughed. "You don't look like a Harold."

"I don't think I look like a Chip."

"Actually, you kind of do."

"Maw-Maw gave me that name."

"She's a good woman."

"The best," Jonas said. "So is Joe. He's a good guy with sound advice. It was driving me crazy about the passenger in the car. For the first few days I was feeling so guilty because I thought the guy died. I still think he is the key to what happened."

"Maybe not a key to what happened that night, but more so what is happening now?" Grant asked.

"Sounds like something Joe would say."

"Do you think it was Jesus in the car with you that night?"

"Sometimes I do. Sometimes I don't. I think the not believing side of me is understanding because who are we to assume we are worthy of Him being there," Jonas said. "Bottom line is, I survived when I shouldn't have. I feel a happiness I don't recognize, happiness which my memory feelings say are new. I believe one way or another He was there."

"I believe that too." Grant stopped at his truck. "Well, goodnight."

"Goodnight."

Grant got in the truck and slowly turned around so he could keep watching Jonas. His son walked to the house next door to the church and sat right on the porch with Pastor Rick.

A slight twinge of jealousy hit him, but it quickly passed.

Grant wanted to be the one on that porch, talking and spending time with Jonas. He wanted to absorb every moment with son, take it all in, just in case when Jonas remembered who he was, he would leave behind who he had become.

TWENTY-TWO

The aroma was amazing in Baker's Market, it always was. In the mornings it was baked goods, and in the afternoon it was the lunch specials. Russ loved the smell in there. It made him hungrier, but on this day, he had other plans for lunch.

Even with big chain stores a short drive away, the people of Williams Peak loved Baker's. They always had everything and rarely ran out of stock.

In fact, the one year there was a toilet paper shortage, and it seemed the whole country went bonkers over stocking up toilet paper.

When it all went down, it just so happened to be the week Marge and Joe had closed down for a few days for a funeral. Not only did they have toilet paper, Marge was the tissue police.

She rationed it out and kept it off the shelves in the back. She broke down packs and sold rolls separately and if you didn't have identification you were from Williams Peak, she said they were out.

They never ran out.

"Look at you," Marge greeted him at the lunch counter. "Didn't recognize you out of uniform."

"I'm always out of uniform when I'm not working."

"You look spiffy," Marge told him. "Are you taking the wife out?"

"No. I have errands to run. That's why I'm here. It's hot out today, hotter than I'd like for June. I wanted to get one of the tea coolers you do. Large please, lemon lime."

"Sure thing. We have Fiesta Turkey Wraps today."

"No, I'm good, I ..." Russ' eyes caught the display. Two for a dollar cookies in a tiny bag. "Chip's chips?" Russ asked.

"Oh, yeah, he was in here bright and early baking. He made other stuff, but those are melt in your mouth, the best cookies you have ever eaten. He's in the back. Did you want to see him?"

"No. No. I'm good. Just impressed. Cookies, huh?"

"Since you're the law." She handed him one. "On me. Let me get that drink."

"Is this a onetime thing?" Russ asked, opening the bag.

Marge worked on the beverage with her back to him, occasionally glancing over her shoulder, and speaking louder as the blender ran. "Pastor Rick only has it in his budget to have him work three days a week. And most of that is room and board. He's only getting a few bucks there."

Russ took a bite of the cookie. The moment he tasted it his mouth lit up with delight. "This is amazing."

"Isn't it? Quite a gift," Marge said. "So, he'll be here a couple days a week baking. He had to learn the bread, but he picked it up right away."

"Well, tell him I think these are fantastic."

"I will. I hope we can get him on more." Marge returned with the drink. "It's on me."

"Thanks."

"Keep an eye out for folks hiring in town, please. He likes the Pastor, but he wants to be able to get his own place. I was thinking of the Sanderson's building, they have those cute places there."

"Marge ..."

"We'd have to take him furniture shopping, decorate it. But then again, you know people in this town. Always throwing good things out. He won't have to worry about food."

"Marge, you do realize once he remembers who he is or learns, he might not stay here."

All expression dropped from Marge's face, then she caught herself and smiled. "Of course."

Russ took the beverage. "But you never know. This is a great town, Marge, so ... you never know. Thank you again."

He grabbed a straw, poked it in and took a drink. It was by far the most refreshing beverage to have on a hot day.

When he stepped outside, he nearly ran over Doc Jenner.

"Look at you," Doc Jenner said. "All spiffy."

"Why is this the second time today I heard those exact same words?"

"Because you are." Doc Jenner motioned his hand up and down. "Jeans, black tee shirt. No hat and, you combed your hair."

"You're out of uniform, too," Russ said.

"I'm off today."

"Oh, good. I was about to go get a burger and wings. New place, you want to join me?"

"That sounds great. Mind if I get one of those drinks first?'

"Sure. Meet you at my car."

"New place, huh?"

"Yep." Russ nodded. "A new place."

Doc Jenner stopped walking the second they approached the place. Russ wondered if he even noticed, he hadn't said anything when they pulled up.

Sure enough, he hesitated walking in.

"Thought you said it was a new place?" Doc Jenner shook his head. "The Rat-Tat-Tat. Are the burgers that good here or is there a reason you have to come out here?"

"A little birdie told me a certain guy has his lunch here every Friday."

"Certain guy meaning the drug dropper?" Jenner asked.

"That's the one."

"This isn't your jurisdiction, Russ. You're not just out of your area, you're way out of your area."

"I just want to talk to the guy."

"How will you know him?"

"The little birdie gave me a picture." Russ pulled out his

phone and showed Doc Jenner.

"Doesn't look like the type to drop a drug in someone's drink."

Russ nodded, agreeing the clean cut guy, average built and looks didn't fit the part. But then as the old saying went, a book can not be judged by the cover.

"This guy. We think he drugged Chip's drink. If he did, he's a piece of work and is not gonna say anything to you. You know that, right?"

"Jenner, you think I'm dumb?" Russ scoffed. "I know well enough this guy isn't going to break easily."

Doug Redding broke down and cried.

Almost instantly and with no prodding.

He was seated at a corner table alone when Russ approached him. He told him who he was and he wasn't there in any legal capacity. He said he just wanted to ask Doug, "Did you know anything about that guitar player who was drugged."

That was when the man lost it.

Russ had seen it a hundred times as a police officer. Someone holding on to guilt, just waiting for the moment they could let it go.

It took Doug a minute, hands over his face, muffled words of, "I'm sorry. I'm so sorry."

"You did it?" Russ asked. "You spiked the drink?"

Doug lowered his hands with a hard sniffle. "I did."

Doc Jenner sat back. "Huh. Well, that was easy."

Russ stayed calm. "What would make you do it?"

"The guys and I were talking. We were mad Lance got kicked out when it was the guitar player who was such a jerk."

Russ nodded. "Still no reason."

"I know."

Doc Jenner asked. "I mean, you had to know what that drug would do. Didn't it dawn on you he was driving?"

Doug shook his head. "No. No it didn't. I thought the band all rode together. I knew they were from out of town. I felt bad about it, but thought he was okay. I didn't know he was in an accident until Chelsey told me his father was in here. She said someone was coming to talk to me today. I'm not running. I admit it."

"I appreciate you admitting it," Russ said.

"Are you going to arrest me?"

"I can't do that. I will turn this over to the state police and see what they want to do. It's a federal offense what you did. It could spell big trouble if they pursue it."

"I know."

"So ... you just found out about the accident? Two days ago?" Russ asked.

Doug nodded.

"You didn't follow him? Pull him from the car, take his guitar?"

"No, sir. Like I said I just found out about the accident."

"I can pull the footage where the guitar was pawned," Russ said.

"It won't be me."

"Thank you." Russ stood. "Doc."

Doc Jenner nodded to Doug and stood. They inched away from the table, speaking in low voices.

"Russ, you had a great theory. I'm sorry it didn't pan out."

"I am, too," Russ said. They sat at a table a good distance from Doug.

"What now?" Jenner asked.

"Now we get our burgers, I'll contact the state police later. At least he admitted it. That still doesn't tell me who the passenger was though, I still believe once we find him, we will know who pawned that guitar."

"Is it important?" Jenner asked.

"Absolutely." Russ gave a firm nod. "He walked away from an accident scene. Had Joe and Marge not shown up he could have been killed."

"He wasn't. We know who he is. We can get the guitar. Seems like you're chasing a tail."

"No. I'm just trying to finish this puzzle." Russ lifted his hand signaling to the bartender they wanted to order.

Doc Jenner smiled with a closed mouth to him. Russ had it in his head he was going to solve the mystery of the passenger with some logical explanation. Jenner wondered if Russ considered the possibility there wasn't a logical explanation, and perhaps never would be.

To an outsider or someone who didn't know the situation, it probably looked stalkerish. Grant admitted to himself it was a little. Hanging back at the market, staying behind a shelf, but watching Jonas as he worked the café for Marge.

Grant had his reasons for being in Baker's Market. Yes, he wanted to take pictures of the cookies, but he also wanted to grab a sandwich to eat before he and Jonas rehearsed that night.

He snapped the pictures and did like he had done with the recording of practice a couple days before … he sent them to Cate.

They had spoken, but the conversations were chilly and brief. She asked about Jonas but didn't want details.

It was as if she had put up this protective front. Grant didn't blame her; he didn't want to get his hopes built up either. How many times in the past did Jonas swear he would change and he didn't? Cate saw it as the same behavior because she refused to believe he had amnesia.

He did.

Grant was convinced. It didn't make it easier or better he didn't remember who he was. There was still a chance once Jonas remembered, he would just say, "I'm out." And find the nearest bar.

Maybe it was silly he sent her pictures. But she hadn't yet

commented on anything he sent her. He just wanted Cate to see what he was seeing. What she had said would happen to Jonas all along. Take him out of his element, away from his friends, and he would change.

Doing his stalker thing, pretending to browse, Grant nearly jumped from his skin when his phone rang. He looked down, saw the name, Jessie, smiled and answered. "Hey, Jess."

"Hey, Daddy. Where are you?" she asked.

"Williams Peak."

"I know that. But where?"

"I'm in the market. Why?"

"Oh, okay, I see it. I'm at some coffee shop called Roasters."

Grant spun. "You're here?"

"Me and Brandon took a ride. He was off today."

"Stay there. I'll be right over." Grant said excitedly. He knew he had told Jessie they weren't telling Jonas who he was yet. He guessed she came to see for herself and maybe be the trigger of memory her brother needed.

He slipped from the store and crossed the street. He saw his son in law sitting at an outside table and Jessie was standing behind him. She waved to Grant and he hurriedly crossed the street.

After shaking Brandon's hand, Grant embraced his daughter.

"This is a surprise, Jess."

"I figured if I wanted to see my father, I better come here. That last text you sent, I took it as you aren't leaving until he remembersd."

"I'm not."

"I understand."

"Are you staying?" Grant asked.

"No, we just did a day trip."

Grant chuckled. "Awfully long drive for a day trip."

"I want to see him, Daddy. Between you saying he doesn't remember and Mom saying he's faking. I need to see for myself. I'll know."

"I know you will. You'll tell your mother, right?"

"I will. But … she's really being stubborn right now about this," Jessie said. "I don't know if she'll listen."

"Well, let's go back to the market and you can see for yourself."

"Sounds good." Jessie grabbed his hands. "How are we going to do this?"

It took a few minutes for Grant to come up with a plan. The three of them going in at once, standing together probably wasn't the best thing to do. Grant worried it could trigger a reaction the doctor had warned about.

The plan was simple, they'd all be in the Market, but separately.

Jonas was working in the café.

Grant went first and ordered his sandwich and a beverage.

"It'll only be a minute," Jonas told him.

Between taking 'to go' orders, Jonas stocked and straightened the café bakery shelves.

While waiting for his sandwich, Grant sat down at a table where he could watch and hear it all.

Brandon came in first. He looked left to right, spotted Jonas and approached. "Excuse me," he said to Jonas. "Do you know where I can find the green olives?"

Jonas turned around. "Condiments, I think. Aisle one."

"Thank you."

Jonas nodded and returned to work.

Nothing. Not a flinch.

Behind Jonas, unseen, Brandon walked backwards, lifting his hands and shrugging.

In came Jessie.

If anyone was going to trigger him, it would be her. She strolled along the counter. Grant saw a reaction, but not from Jonas.

Jessie couldn't hide the fact she was overwhelmed seeing her little brother and shocked by how he looked.

"Can I help you?" he asked as she stood at the counter.

"Um ..." Jessie just stared at him.

"Miss?"

"Oh, hey, yeah, wow. These cookies look great."

"I made them. Chip's Chips. I'm Chip."

"They look so good."

"Did you want to buy some?"

"No. I mean. Yes. That was rude." She pulled out a bill and put it on the counter.

"Would you like anything else?" he asked. "We have great tea smoothies."

"Look at you upselling, I'm impressed."

"Excuse me?"

"Listen," she leaned into the counter. "I'm passing through town. Is there a place where I can get a drink? Maybe when you're done ..."

Jonas chuckled almost shyly, shaking his head.

"What?" she asked.

"Look, you seem nice and all. But ... I kind of am interested in someone right now. But thanks." He turned to the window behind the counter and grabbed a bag.

Jessie's jaw dropped. She stammered a few words that were more like noises.

"Mr. Truett?" Jonas called. "Your sandwich is done."

Jessie stormed away.

Trying to hide his laugh, Grant approached the counter for his bag. "What was that about?"

"Oh, she was hitting on me."

"Can't have that."

"No, I can't, plus ..." Jonas crinkled his face. "She gave off this weird vibe. Who knows? Maybe it's me."

"No, I don't think so." Grant held up the bag. "Thanks. See you tonight."

It took everything Grant had not to burst out laughing, he found the encounter amusing.

Jessie didn't. She was angry when he returned to find her at the coffee shop.

"He said I was hitting on him," Jessie said. "I just thought, maybe mention drinking..."

Grant nodded. "Went right over his head."

Jessie folded her arms. "He looks really good."

"I know."

"Mom needs to see him.

"What's your verdict?" Grant asked. "Team Mom or Team Dad."

"Team Jonas," Jessie replied. "And he's not here."

"You believe the amnesia?"

"One hundred percent, but Dad, as much as he looks great, is happy, that is not my brother," Jessie said. "And sadly, the Jonas we all know will return."

TWENTY-THREE

It was a pattern he had seen before, but Grant just could not remember where. A figure eight, chain link design. Grant couldn't name the type of flowers they were. Yellow ones made up the 'eight', pink ones all surrounding. The design ran from the side of the church to the front, repeatedly.

Quietly, Grant took a picture. He didn't want to be 'too much' and was worried Jonas in his amnesiac state would think he was a creepy old guy. He had spent the entire evening practicing with Jonas, spending all the time he could with him. Jessie's words stayed heavily on his mind.

In short, she was saying enjoy him while he could because once Jonas remembered, Chip would be gone.

"Mr. Truett?" the soft woman's voice called.

Grant jumped a little and turned. "Oh, Haley, sorry."

"I saw you standing there. Everything alright?"

"I'm just taking pictures."

"Beautiful isn't it?"

"I've seen it before," Grant said. "This exact pattern."

"Then he created this before?" Haley asked.

"I'm not sure. I don't remember it being here a couple days ago."

"It wasn't. Chip has been working on it constantly."

"I just wanted to take pictures. I've been documenting everything, sending it to my wife."

"Is she enjoying them?"

Grant shrugged. "I don't know. She doesn't comment on them. She doesn't believe our son has amnesia."

"There are times, every now and then, that I wonder if he knows who he is. Maybe just not wanting to admit it. Then I see that look in his eye and I know, he has no clue. He's lost. You can't fake the look of wonder."

"What do you mean?"

"It's like he's a baby that's seeing so much for the first time. Maybe your wife will know that pattern."

"Maybe. I really should get going. I don't want him to see me hanging around."

"Can I ask why?" Haley questioned.

"Because the last thing I want is for him to think I'm weird and to then back off. I'm just so in awe of him right now, I can't get enough. He always loved music, it brought him so much joy. But not like this."

"Again, it's that baby thing I was telling you about. But it's okay. No one thinks you're weird. Chip will not think that. I promise. And it's understandable. You were so worried about him, missing him. It's your son."

"Is it?"

"Yes." Haley tilted her head. "Is there anything about the way he acts that is like the Jonas you know?"

Grant chuckled. "Maybe when he was twelve. When we got him that guitar he was so sure he was going to be a rock star and famous. Everyone was going to sing his songs." Grant smiled. "When he was a kid, he had this naivety about him. Such an innocence. I loved that about him. His innocence. Every other kid was wanting to grow up so fast, but not Jonas, he loved being a kid. He did things for people. Was upbeat and happy."

"Sounds awfully familiar, doesn't it?"

"Yeah, I guess it does. You know, we searched for answers." Grant looked down at the flowers. "Trying to find a reason why Jonas just flipped a switch. Some traumatic experience we didn't know about. But … that's not how it works. Sometimes the best kids can get caught up in some bad stuff."

Haley nodded. "I have known a few. It's a disease."

"Yes, it is."

"What was he like? The Jonas that went and disappeared?"

"You know ... I'm not going to tell you. I'll leave that for him. My son, he likes you. You're a very nice woman, Haley. Maybe I shouldn't have said anything."

"No, I like him, too. And you're right, you're absolutely right for not telling me. I don't want to judge Chip on who he was before he can remember it."

"Exactly. And again, I should go before he sees me lurking."

"He's not here. He's at the field. It's the weekly softball game."

"My son ... is playing softball?" Grant asked.

"You sound surprised."

"Yes, he never played sports in his life."

Haley laughed. "No wonder he's so bad. He hits well, can't catch worth a squat."

"I tried to teach him. He just wasn't interested."

"Do you play softball?" Haley asked.

"I did when the kids were young. He used to come to all the games."

"Why don't you join us?"

"Oh, no, I can't. Me showing up would just be awkward."

Haley laughed and smiled brightly. "Mr. Truett, welcome to Williams Peak. You're a newcomer in town. I would have sought you out today anyhow."

"Really? Can you find me a glove?"

"We can do that. Let's go." She started walking backwards.

"Haley, can you do me a favor?"

"Sure."

"Can you take some pictures?"

"For your wife?"

Grant nodded. "I want her to see."

"Then absolutely, I will."

Grant thanked her. He'd follow her in his truck to the field, wherever that happened to be. He was happy and excited to be there. He wouldn't be able to take the photos and was glad Haley agreed to it. If anything was going to convince Cate Jonas had amnesia, watching him play sports would be the thing.

"It's not a figure eight," Cate spoke softly to herself looking at the pictures Grant had sent. He asked in a text about the figure eight garden and where he had seen it.

Cate just shook her head. How did he not remember?

She wanted to reply, but it was late. Grant was probably in bed, she had already ignored replying for hours, it was pointless now.

It frustrated her Grant didn't know, didn't recall it.

It wasn't a figure eight, it was an infinity symbol.

When she saw the picture, she was even more convinced Jonas didn't have amnesia. The colors, the shape, it was all an exact replica of a garden her and Jonas had planted years before.

Many years.

He was fourteen.

Why that garden? Why redo it?

The day she showed him the design, he thought it was cool. It was going to be difficult, but Cate explained to Jonas it was a symbol of never ending. Like the loop kept going, so would the beauty of the garden.

It was a huge project she and Jonas took on that summer.

He had such a gift with gardening, she had savored every moment they did something together.

There she was, seventeen years later looking at a picture taken hours earlier that could have been taken over a decade before.

And yet, there she was on a Saturday night, staring at the beauty of it, seeing the garden and again, like every weekend night, her mind became occupied with thoughts of Jonas.

Only this night it wasn't worry or concern, it was confusion.

Even more so was the confusion while Cate was having her dinner, a number she didn't know, started sending her images and videos.

Hi, your husband asked me to send these to you.

At first, she wondered who was this poor person Grant had pulled into Jonas' web with him?
Then she watched.
Cate watched the video over and over.
It spoke volumes in more ways than one.

The 'clunk' sound as the ball hit the bat, followed by a cheer of a crowd. The person recording was a female, young, guessing by the voice when she first heard it.
"Woo. Go Mr. Truett."
The video badly zoomed in and out as Grant ran the bases for a double.

Cate smiled, he looked so happy and even looked young. A part of her envied Grant for just going with it. For embracing some sort of chance he thought was long gone or he'd never see again.
A closeness with Jonas he had avoided for many years.
It was undeniable, even by Grant, that his choice of 'Tough love' with Jonas was what had driven him to look for him until he found him

The camera turned showing a beautiful young woman doing a selfie recording. Her brown hair in a sloppy ponytail. "We're playing Crossroads Church today. Mr. Truett just drove in what could be the winning run. Oh, wait. Chip is up."
Chip?
Then Cate saw Jonas at bat. The first time she watched the video, her heart literally skipped a beat. He was wearing shorts, longer ones, but his calves didn't look like matchsticks and if she wasn't mistaken, he had a little bit of a belly. It had to be the shirt.
Jonas hit the ball and carried that bat halfway to first base. The

girl cheered and Jonas kept running, trying to get a double like his
father, but he was thrown out at second base after doing what Cate
believed was the worst slide she had ever seen.

"It's Okay Chip! You tried."

She laid on the top of her bed, the phone in her hand, looking at the pictures over and over. Cate truly tried to justify why
she was still at home. Why she wasn't there cheering in the
bleachers?

Cate didn't have it in her to be broken again.

How many times had she been pulled into that scheme? The
'I'm better and stronger' act that turned on a dime more times
than she could count.

She wasn't angry at Grant; in fact, she was happy he was having fun.

Oddly, Cate carried a sense of peace at that moment, an
ability to relax without needing Sleepy Time tea. Much like the
nights Jonas was arrested. Instantly she didn't worry about that
middle of the night phone call saying he was dead. She knew he
was safe, albeit in jail.

Now he was safe again, his father nearby. Deep in some
Nebraska small town, baking cookies, creating gardens, playing
music and playing on a church softball team.

A part of Cate knew it from the moment he vanished he
was okay. She had that connection to him, and it was that connection that convinced her, Jonas was only one step away from
doing it again.

Throwing all caution, and his life, to the wind to live on the
edge.

Even with Jessie telling her the amnesia was real, Cate just
didn't buy it. She knew her son too well.

Or she just didn't want to believe it.

Perhaps it was the fact of what she witnessed in the pictures,
videos and texts was the wish of every mother of a wayward
child. To see that child grow, change, find peace and be happy.

It was all a fairytale Grant was being pulled into and Cate

had to resist, because like all fairytales, eventually they all would come to an end.

TWENTY-FOUR

The coffee was good, Cate didn't expect it to be. She took small sips because it stayed hot in her travel mug. The bench was comfortable enough for her and the weather was mild enough to enjoy sitting outside.

She wished she would stop having bad memories. Memories that made her angry or convinced Jonas stint in Williams Peak wasn't some spiritual rehab, but rather some twisted con. Why did she lack so much faith in her son? A change of tides. Now Grant was the one who had faith, not only in Jonas, but real faith.

It was the first Sunday in years she had missed services. In a sense, she reasoned she wasn't. Her mind did drift to one of those bad moment memories. Nothing anyone else would see as major, Cate did.

She had gone to a resale bookstore and found an oversized, beautiful, hardback book of Charlton Heston bible interpretations. She was excited about it, had even showed Jonas.

Instead of saying, "Oh, cool." The young man who skirted death, who Cate felt should have dropped to his knees and been grateful he was alive, instead said, "Why do you believe in that crap?"

"There's no God, certainly not like you think."

He said that adamantly. She often wondered if he had said them because he really believed it or only to hurt Cate. Saying hurtful things to her was not unusual.

People in the support group would tell her, "Oh, it's not him talking, it's the alcohol or the drugs."

Cate didn't believe them, she believed truth came out of

mouths when the mind was full of substance.

Maybe she was wrong.

She sat on that bench, thinking of the day he claimed to not believe while staring at a church, where her son was inside playing music and singing.

She wasn't going to go in. In fact, she arrived a couple days earlier than she told Grant. Slipped into Williams Peak quietly and unnoticed, or so she thought.

"I thought he mumbled," the gentleman said as he sat next to her on the bench.

"The pastor, I thought he mumbled a little at the end."

"Um, yeah, he did. I had a hard time hearing."

"We're sitting outside." He extended his hand. "Joe. Some call me Old Joe. I'm gonna bet, call it a hunch, that you're Cate Truett."

"I am. You're good."

"Nah, we just don't get strangers much. So … are you here for the revealing?"

Cate nodded. "Tuesday is exactly a month. Grant said they're going to tell him. I want to be here for that. He doesn't know they're telling him, does he?"

Joe shook his head. "No. He thinks he's gonna do a fingerprint with the chief. I'm glad you came."

"People who know don't think I'm a horrible mother for not showing up, do they?'

Joe laughed. "No. Plus, I think Grant has been having the time of his life with him."

"It seems so. I'm not a cold person, I love my son. It was hard to come here."

"I get it. I do. Your son has amnesia, he wouldn't know you anyhow, right?"

"Does he?"

"Yes, he does. Look," Joe said. "The wife and I had an inkling about your boy, Grant confirmed it. I like to consider myself an expert in men like your son. People that took the wrong path. I know your reluctance. I know how easy it is to jump on the thought he is manipulating everyone. But I will say he isn't. Besides, when you meet Pastor Rick, don't be fooled by how nice he is. He's smart as a whip when it comes to this. I can remember him telling me and my wife not to be fooled by our son. He knew every time Matthew wasn't clean."

"I probably won't meet him," Cate said.

"You will. So, why did you come early if you only want to hang in the shadows?"

"I didn't want to miss something I might not get a chance to ever see again," Cate explained. "It's the wish of every parent of an addict that their child will one day see the light, stop using, stop drinking, walk the straight path. I know it happens, but I just don't see Jonas there yet."

"You haven't seen him in a month. You haven't seen what we have, what Grant has."

"I know. That's why I'm here, once he knows, he'll probably never pick up his guitar for Christ again."

"You don't know that," Joe said. "None of us do."

"He's going to be mad. Not when we tell him, but when he remembers. When Jonas comes back. When hot-headed Jonas comes back, he is going to be livid about living this life."

"I don't think Chip disappears when Jonas comes back. Not sure amnesia works that way, Joe said. "But I have to agree he might be mad. Mad at himself for making wrong choices. Mad at himself maybe for the way he was."

"So, you've been there?" Cate asked.

"I have. Very similar circumstances, the outcome not as good. Our son fought with us one night. You know the drill, the intervention, trying to help. He disappeared. For weeks we couldn't find him. Then we did. He was walking. Heavily under the influence. He fell, got hurt and died right there buried in the brush."

"Oh, oh, Joe, I am so sorry."

"Thank you." Joe reached over and grabbed her hand. "But we are grateful for your son. Cate, he gave us a chance to reconcile our feelings about our own son. He has helped my wife and

I more than you or he realized. By us being there for him, helping him, we had a second chance. And let me tell you, he's made changes."

"Like what?"

"See all of them cars for Sunday service? A month ago, there were ten cars. He's brought the service up so much that people come here. The Chief. He has been chasing this passenger in the car with your son. I haven't seen him have a purpose in a long time. Look at the church garden. It's alive. Listen to the music Cate. I like it. No, I love it."

"It sounds wonderful."

"Bet it sounds better inside. What do you say we go in for the reprise? I really liked that song. I'm interested in hearing it closer." Joe stood and held out his hand. "We'll sit in the back. No one will see us. Let's go hear your son and watch him play."

Cate took his hand and stood. She set her coffee cup on the bench.

They started walking towards the church, the pastor was speaking over the soft music. Which told Cate he was wrapping up.

Joe stopped walking just before he entered the church. "Well, how about that. I just thought of another thing your son has done."

"What's that?"

"When I lost my own boy, I stopped going to service. I said I would never walk into a Sunday Service again. The anger in me, thinking those praying, weren't praying hard enough for my boy. Yet, here I am, about to go in because of your boy."

"Thank you, Joe. Thank you so much."

Joe smiled for her and opened the door.

The music increased in volume and sounded so much better than outside. It wasn't an upbeat song, it was a reflection one. The woman who sang was older and truly expelled the power and emotions behind the music.

Joe inched her forward a few pews and pointed. A woman in the row turned. Her face seemed to light up when she saw Joe, and when Cate saw her smile, she knew it was the woman they called Maw-Maw.

Haley sent several pictures of Jonas and Maw-Maw. In fact, the young woman communicated frequently with Cate. It wasn't a guilt thing, she just wanted to give her updates.

Had she not, she would have been shocked when she saw her son on that stage.

He didn't really face the congregation too much, too busy watching the other members, giving directions with a nod.

Jonas not only looked happy, he looked healthy. She thought instantly of the one text and picture she got from Haley. 'Day twenty-two, flavor twenty-two, peanut butter mint.'

Jonas was enjoying himself, Cate cringed.

A part of her felt like she was picking up her son from rehab, one she prayed would work.

And there was a change in Grant. She hadn't seen him look this happy or stress free in forever. It had also been years since she saw Grant play anything other than a few Christmas songs at get togethers.

Cate sat back and enjoyed watching her family. She was glad she made the decision to come early. If it all changed when Jonas remembered who he was, she didn't want to miss her chance of experiencing it.

"What an uplifting day this is," Pastor Rick stepped center altar, holding the microphone and a hand behind his back. "We learned a lot didn't we? Thank you for coming today, for worshiping with us and remember ... When you let it go, just as fast ..." he raised his hidden hand. It wore a baseball glove. And no sooner did he lift it, a ball sailed across the altar from Grant and Pastor Rick caught it. "God takes it." Pastor Rick said. "I have to tell you. We practiced that, but still ... I was afraid I'd miss." He looked at Grant.

"Me, too," Grant said.

The congregation laughed.

"God doesn't miss, though," Pastor Rick said. "Have a great

week, be good to one another, and remember, you are loved. Please rise and sing praises with our band."

The intro to the song fell on the shoulders of Grant and Jonas.

Jonas counted it off quietly to the drummer, turned to face the congregation and stepped to the microphone, when he did something that was rare for him. He struck a wrong chord.

It was obvious and really off. Jonas had a frozen expression on his face.

Pastor Rick covered. "Guess the band is a little stunned by my athletics."

Grant mouthed the words to Jonas, "What's wrong?"

Jonas shook his head and stared at Grant.

Looking at the drummer, Grant counted the song again. This time Jonas played correctly. He missed the first chord of the introduction but jumped in and caught up.

The song was upbeat and uplifting, Jonas sang as if he had to concentrate on every word. The end of the song was music with the four person backup singers, taking the chorus as the musical instruments in the band took it home.

Something was up, Grant didn't know what it was, but Jonas looked odd on stage.

He stared at Grant, then made his way over toward the keyboard, playing and jamming the last part of the song.

When the last note played, after Jonas' hand struck downward across the string, he lifted the guitar strap over his head, and handed the guitar to Grant. "Thank you."

He sounded different. Grant realized why when Jonas spun, raced down half the steps, jumped the rest of the way and called out, "Mom!"

Cate had made her way out of her seat and into the side aisle. The song was over, and she wanted to leave and go back to the hotel. Her back turned, she heard it.

"Mom."

Not only did she stop, but her heart did, too. She looked up. "Mom!"

She hurriedly turned around, listening to the emotional call of her name, she didn't move. How could she, she could barely breathe.

Jonas pushed his way through, calling for her, His eyes finally making contact with Cate a few feet before he drew close.

Jonas stopped, his shoulders bounced up and down. His face red and eyes glossed over with emotions. "Mom." His voice cracked.

Then in one long stride he reached out to her.

Cate grabbed onto him; she clutched her son close. She was strong, holding it together, until she heard him weep. Grabbing on to her like a lost little boy.

"I'm sorry. I'm so sorry, Mom. I'm so sorry. I'm sorry."

Throat tightening, Cate choked on any words that could possibly come out. All she could do was hold on to him, cry with relief and joy. Her legs felt too weak to stand. She wasn't letting go of him, not out of their embrace, not yet, maybe never.

Haley watched. She sat behind the board when it happened. She wasn't the only one who heard it, it seemed everyone, especially those who knew Chip's situation, just stopped. Hand over her mouth, she had watched Jonas push through the crowd, calling out, over and over. "Mom! Mom!" until he found her, grabbed her and held out.

Haley knew the reason he froze on stage. There was no doubt.

The moment Jonas saw his mother, he remembered.

He remembered it all.

TWENTY-FIVE

It wasn't like he believed it would happen. Jonas had seen amnesia portrayed in movies and television before. It wasn't some big giant wave of memories and suddenly he was alright. It was bit by bit, then blast. And the memories that came first weren't good. They were arguments with his parents, things he had said, ugly things. The memories that had probably kept him from remembering.

Everyone attributed it to his mother triggering his memory. But it wasn't. It was his father.

Something about the look he gave Jonas from across the stage, just before the song started. It caused some voice inside his head to remember his name and recognize Grant as his father.

It was then he turned around, finding Maw-Maw to focus on and he saw his mother.

He had to close his eyes to play, to sing the song, to believe the words, because the entire time he sang, the memories kept coming.

He raced from that stage wanting only to hug her. Somewhere though in their emotional reunion, he passed out.

Waking up in the emergency room.

The feeling was strange, his time in Williams Peak, suddenly knowing how it felt to not remember who he was.

It wasn't just relief that hit Jonas, worry, fear and regret came along for the ride.

How would they look at him? Jonas wasn't just seeing Haley, Pastor Rick, Maw-Maw and Joe the way he did, as Chip anymore. A blank page was filled in.

They weren't strangers to him, as he expected would happen when the memory returned. They were family, and just like he felt with his mom and dad, he wondered if he was worthy enough to be around them.

After being so good for so long, sitting there on that hospital examining table, alone in the room, Jonas felt like a fraud.

Doc Jenner slid open the glass door and stepped inside. "Good news, everything looks good."

"I'm fine, I don't understand why you had to run all those tests."

"One ... you passed out. You had trauma and I wanted to make sure everything was working as it should. Getting your memory back affects you physically."

"I'm fine."

"I know. Do you feel like you're still missing anything?" Doc Jenner asked.

"The accident. I mean, I remember my drummer handing me my phone because it fell on the floor. My mom ..." He forcefully exhaled. "My mom had texted, and I blew them off."

"Do you remember the accident?"

"Same as before, the guy in the car. I can see him clearer now though. I remember him being in the car when I got in. Then after the windshield thing ... nothing. Nothing until Ann the nurse was with me the next morning."

"Well, unfortunately, a lot of that had to do with the drug in your system. That causes black outs."

Jonas nodded.

"I'll get you all signed out. You have people waiting in the waiting room to make sure you're alright," Doc Jenner said. "Why don't you go see them?"

Jonas didn't reply.

"Are you all right?"

"Yeah. Just ... it feels weird now, that's all." Jonas slid from the table and walked to the door. "Thank you."

"You're welcome," Doc Jenner replied. "And I'm glad your memory is back."

It wasn't that long of a wait, an hour or so, Grant lost track of time. He was nervous about being at the hospital, seeing Jonas all over.

Doc Jenner told them he believed Jonas was fine and was waiting on the results. That was the last Grant heard. He sat in the waiting room with Cate, Marge, Joe and Haley. They were the only ones there, the emergency room wasn't busy at all.

He wondered how much Jonas remembered. Everything? Only a little?

Two cups of coffee later, Jonas came from the back through the doors.

Everyone stood.

"Are you all right?" Cate rushed to him.

"Yeah, I think I need to take a walk."

"Maybe, it's not a good idea," Cate said. "One of us could go with you…"

"I'm fine."

"Or…"

"Mom!" Jonas snapped. "I'm fine."

It was a bolt of shock that went through Grant when he heard the tone to Jonas' voice. "We're just worried, Jonas."

"Worried enough to lie to me?" he asked. "You spent all that time with me. Hanging around and not once did you tell me who you are. How could you do that to me? Huh? Did you hate me that much, hate who I was, that you just wanted to pretend I was someone brand new? Or better yet, maybe you wanted me never to remember?"

"Don't …" Marge softly scolded. "Don't blame him. Do not put the blame on them. You want to blame someone. Blame me. I believed you didn't want to know until you remembered. Now you do. Nobody wanted to lie to you. I was just going by what you said."

"You're right, I did say that. I … have to take a walk." Shaking his head, Jonas walked out of the emergency room in a storming manner.

"And just like that." Cate said softly. "The old Jonas comes back."

"Please don't say that," Haley said. "Please believe in him." She turned and hurried to catch up to Jonas.

Cate closed her eyes and sat back down. "That ... that was wrong of me to say."

Marge sat next to her. "I know it's hard. But I truly think he's just confused. Imagine ... this morning he woke up one person and in the middle of service he remembers not only who he was, but a person he thinks is completely opposite of the Chip that was working at the church."

"Isn't he?" Cate asked.

"No." Marge shook her head. "He's not a different person. He just got a chance to bring a part of him out that he buried. Have faith." Marge squeezed her hand. "I do."

Haley found him.

He was standing outside on the sidewalk into front of Jumping Jupiter Bar and Grill.

Just standing there. She didn't know if he was staring inside or debating on whether to go in.

After a few moments of debate on whether to approach him, Haley darted across the street and stood next to him. "Boy, for someone who just got out of the hospital, you run fast."

He glanced at her through the reflection in the glass. "It's all that softball you had me doing."

Haley softly chuckled, then drew seriously. "Are you all right?"

"Yeah. Just thinking. Looking."

"Inside? It's not that great. Are you mad at me?"

"You? No. Never."

Haley smiled. "Thank you."

"You know this is my social media name?"

"Jumping Jupiter?"

Jonas chuckled. "Just Jupiter. My way of hiding from my family. They couldn't find out. Sound familiar?"

"But they did find you here in Williams Peak, and I'm willing to bet they found you on social media, too. You just didn't know it."

"I didn't mean to be so hard on them back there. Like I always do, I blamed them."

"It's not okay, I'm not going to tell you it was."

"Thank you."

"But they're you're parents. They love you. They'll understand and forgive you."

"How many times, Haley?" he asked. "How many times do I hurt them? Lash out? Before they give up on me."

"They'll never give up on you, even when you give up on yourself. Can I ask why you're staring into Jupiter's? Are you thinking about the loaded fry special?"

"No, but it does sound good with a milkshake." He glanced over to her with a smile. "This is not egotistical. I'm looking at my reflection. Ironically through a window of a bar. Which pretty much defined my lifestyle before the accident. Metaphorically speaking, I'm looking inside myself actually. I look at this reflection. I like who I see, I just don't like who I am or was."

"The nice thing about being one way and not liking it, is you can change it," Haley said.

"Did I change, or did I just become who everyone wanted me to be? I feel like this huge phony."

"You're not. Trust me. Can I be honest with you?

"When aren't you?" Jonas asked.

"True. Maybe deep down, Chip is who you wanted to be."

Jonas grumbled half-jokingly. "Oh, I don't know about that. I doubt it. I wanted to be a rock star."

"In a way you are. In Williams Peak."

"Haley." He faced her. "I used to ridicule my mother for going to church. For believing in God. I'd argue with her about

Him. I'd tell her I didn't believe."

"Maybe you really did and just thought you were too cool to admit it."

Jonas shook his head. "No. No, I didn't believe at all."

"Do you now?"

Jonas softly laughed. "Yeah. I mean how can I deny His existence? Since the accident there's no denying. I'm here, I'm alive, I shouldn't be. Especially when things about the accident and the car are just unanswered."

"The passenger?"

Jonas nodded. "Yes. There's no explanation for him. No answers other than it was divine intervention."

"Would Jonas, a month ago be saying this?" Haley asked.

"No. Absolutely not. No."

"Then how are you a fraud, how can you even ask if you became who everyone wanted you to be? I know that's on your mind. I wish my words could convince you of what I believe."

"Which is?" Jonas asked.

"I believe God gave you a gift of not knowing who you were in your past so you could find who you need to be in the future. I think if you take some time and do some soul searching..." she tilted her head. "Pray on it? Find your answers."

"Not that I don't think prayer isn't powerful, but you're right. I need answers about who I was and about that night, the accident ... the passenger. I think I know where to start."

Haley looked at Jonas curiously.

The two-tone musical alert went off when the door opened, and Russ looked over because he knew someone entered.

He saw Jonas walking in.

"Word on the street has it that someone got their memory back," Russ said.

"Word on the street would be correct."

"I'm happy for you."

"Thanks."

"What can I help you with?" Russ asked, motioning his hand to the chair at his desk.

"Is there anything I can help you with?" Jonas questioned as he took a seat.

"Well, that's nice of you." Russ sat down. "But I don't think you know as much as I do."

Jonas laughed. "You don't say."

"I do say."

"Chief … I know you wanted to find out who I was. I know that. I appreciate you not telling me. I don't think I could have handled knowing how I was."

"Was is the key word." Russ winked. "I like that. Little truth here …" he leaned back in the chair. "Had I run your prints, had I read your rap sheet, I probably wouldn't have told you. I would have called your parents. I like your dad."

"I do, too." Jonas looked down to his folded hands.

"Do you remember anything about that night?"

Jonas shook his head. "Not much. I remember the guy in my car a lot clearer now."

"What did he look like?"

"Thin. Dark hair. It was long, like one length, came to here." Jonas touched below his own shoulder. "Beard, but it wasn't grown too much or shaped. Does that make sense?'

"It does."

"Have you found him?'

Russ shook his head. "Nope. Nothing on him at all."

"Chief, I know you have been working hard on my case, Marge said you were borderline obsessive."

"I was. Am."

"Can I ask why?"

"You can." Russ nodded. "And I'll be honest with you. When I met you, I knew there was trouble around you. Your coloring, your weight, that anger. I wanted to help you. I thought at first if I could do that, I could make up for what I didn't do for Marge and Joe's kid. I didn't look hard enough. I didn't put forth the effort I should have because I thought he'd show up after another binge. But he didn't. I have to live with that. So, in some way, if I could help you, it would be my atonement. Then, it turned into more because I really saw a good kid in you."

"Thank you. Did you learn anything? Anything I don't know?"

"A lot. Not sure if you know it or now. I have dug deep. I can tell you that much."

"Please," Jonas said.

"That night of the accident, you got into an argument with a guy named Lance over his girlfriend. According to witnesses, you egged him on. It got physical, some shoving, he decked you, fight broke up. He tried to apologize but you had him kicked out. After your last set his buddy Doug gave you a bygone be bygones drink."

"It was spiked."

Russ nodded. "Yep. He didn't know you weren't driving with your friends. State Police have been waiting for you to get your memory back to see if you want to press charges. They've charged him anyhow, but if you jump on it, they're gonna up the charge to attempted murder."

Jonas slumped back. "What is he saying about it? This Doug."

"Oh, he's tore up. Wracked with guilt. I thought he was the passenger at first. Or followed you, saw the accident and pulled you out. But he wasn't. I couldn't find anything about the passenger. Not saying I didn't try."

"I appreciate it."

"You had all your gear in that car. The car caught fire. But you had said something to me ..." Russ reached down, grabbed his travel mug and set it on the desk.

Jonas looked at it. "The design. I told you it looked familiar."

"Because of your guitar."

Jonas nodded. 'Yes. The same design."

"Everyone thought I was nuts. But I saw it at Guitar World in Fremont. An eighteen year old kid named Kevin McConnel hocked it for two-hundred and twenty-five bucks."

"It's worth way more than that, monetarily and to me."

"Yes, it is. Kevin swore he found it on the highway. Probably thrown from the car. That's what he said."

"You don't believe him."

Russ lifted his hands. "Nothing I can do. I thought whoever pawned your guitar was your passenger. I thought maybe this passenger survived the crash, took off with your guitar. But I was wrong. I'm probably out of practice because to be honest, this is the first case in a while I really had to solve."

"I appreciate it. You said my guitar was at Guitar World?"

"It was."

"Was? So, it's been sold?"

"Yep." Russ stood up. "Can you excuse me for a second?" He walked over to the closet near his desk and opened it. He pulled out a guitar case. "I know how much finding out who the passenger was means to you. Answers, I can't give you. But I can give you this." He put the case on a table. "I knew you'd get your memory back."

Almost awestruck, Jonas walked to the table. He slowly undid the latches and lifted the lid to the case. When his eyes cast upon it, an ache of a moan flowed from him. He turned his head to Russ with glossed over eyes. "You did this? You got my guitar for me? I can't thank you enough. How much do I owe you?"

"Don't insult me. You owe me nothing. I got that for you. My thank you."

"Thank me?" Jonas asked shocked. "Why are you even thanking me?"

"You helped me heal. After Matthew, I doubted everything I stood for. Helping you got me to believe in myself again. I didn't think that would ever happen."

"I don't deserve this."

"Yes, you do. Now take that guitar. Believe in yourself," Russ said. "Because I believe in you."

◆ ◆ ◆

It was one of those days, they happened every so often, when Pastor Rick would think he wanted to get a dog.

He took a walk, thinking about how nice of a summer evening it was, and if he had a dog, he wouldn't be so bored on a walk.

It was on his way back to the house that he heard it. A sound of guitar playing coming from the church.

He thought he had locked up, maybe he was wrong. Then again, the guitar playing sounded familiar and it could only be one person.

Pastor Rick walked into the church through the side door and onto the stage, where he saw Jonas sitting in the first row. He had an electric guitar on his lap. A cord ran from the guitar to an amp.

It looked like a new guitar. It was semi dark in the church, but he swore the guitar looked like the Chief's travel mug.

Jonas stopped playing when he saw the pastor.

"Don't stop because of me," Pastor Rick said.

"It's okay."

"That sounded beautiful."

"I'm writing a song. Thought I'd process things by putting it to music. My journey and stuff."

"Well, that might be an opus."

Jonas laughed.

"I'm very happy you got your memory back."

"Thank you. And thank you so much for all you've done."

"I have to tell you, I was a little concerned. Haley told me you were upset."

"I was. I was mad. I wasn't nice."

"Haley told me that, too,"

"Yep, and she told me I needed to find answers. I went to the Chief. He gave me some answers."

"Enough to help?" Pastor Rick asked.

"Enough to start."

"What's troubling you?" Pastor Rick looked up and smiled. "Wait. That was so pastor like of me to ask that."

Jonas smiled. "I'm sitting here and holding my guitar. It feels good, right. But playing in here also feels right. In my mind those two things should not feel right together."

"What about in your heart?"

"My heart says, I know who I am, it's time to get back to that life. To that crappy apartment on seventh, cutting grass and playing music."

"Hmm. Sounds kind of like what you do now. Although, I think your room at the house is nice."

"It is."

"Seems to me your day to day didn't change all that much, rather your outlook."

"I had amnesia," Jonas said.

"You did."

"I have to go back. Isn't that the right thing to do?"

"The correct thing is what feels accurate to you. I can imagine a part of you thinks you need to pack up and head back to your old life because you know who you are now."

Jonas nodded. "I feel that."

"When you arrived in our little town and you didn't know who you were, you had an adjustment period, correct? Just like you didn't jump right into being a, hardworking, fun loving, cookie baking nice guy Chip, you don't need to jump right back into being, partying, living on the edge, never happy, jerk of a guy Jonas."

"Wow." Jonas laughed.

"You need an adjustment period. Take it. That's my advice. You know what you want more than you care to admit. I promise. You'll figure it out. Now ..." He clapped his hands once. "Let's hear your opus?"

Jonas smiled and just to have fun, he ripped into a hard core, hard rock riff. Then after saying 'just kidding', he returned to the song he was working on when Pastor Rick came in.

His memory returned and with it came a lot of good advice from everyone who had gotten to know him. But what of the two people in town who knew him his whole life. Talking to them would have to start with an apology long overdue.

TWENTY-SIX

It wasn't the first time she had heard an apology from Jonas, but it was the first time Cate actually felt it was believable.

The night before he called her at the hotel and said, "I'm sorry, Mom. Can we talk? Maybe over a milkshake?."

She and Grant met him at the milkshake shop and Jonas apologized again, not only for the outburst hours earlier at the hospital but for many things.

"I'm sorry for all the sleepless nights. I'm sorry I was mean and hurtful. I'm sorry for destroying my body, for not being the son you raised me to be. I can make a list, I can say I'm sorry, but I don't know what I can do to make it right."

Cate and Grant held him.

"You don't need to make it up to us, Jonas," Grant told him. "We want what's best for you. We want you happy. That life you led, it didn't make you happy. You were searching. And I pray, yes, I pray you don't ever go back."

"But that is your choice," Cate added. "We can't tell you what to do."

He had come to them for answers and advice, and Cate didn't want to tell him what she thought he should do, because it ultimately had to be what he wanted to do, what was in his heart.

One thing was clear, Jonas hadn't left his job at the market bakery. He had done his morning shift, asking Cate and Grant to not leave town yet. If one of them could stay at least, until he made up his mind on what he needed to do.

Grant was still on sabbatical and Cate had to get back to work. One more day and she had to leave. However, she planned on enjoying her time in the quaint town.

"You should stay until Wednesday," Grant told Cate as they sat on the patio of Baker's Market Café. "It's meatball sub day and they are awesome."

"I wish I could. But you know, I think Jonas is going to be ready to leave here in a few days. He knows who he is. Right now, he's getting his phone back."

"We should have cancelled his number," Grant told her.

"Cancelling his number isn't going to cancel his old life."

"Speaking of Jonas." Grant lifted his chin to nod.

The phone store bag seat on the table. "Hey." Jonas pulled up a chair and sat down. "You got the chicken wraps. They're pretty good, huh?"

"You hungry?" Grant pushed his sandwich to him. "There is still half."

"No, Maw-Maw made me eat one about an hour ago."

Cate smiled gently. "She is very good to you."

"Yes, she is. Has been since day one," Jonas stated. "Even when I wasn't easy to be nice to. And I told her I didn't want her help. She didn't listen because she wasn't doing it for me. She was doing it for you, Mom."

"Me?" Cate asked.

Jonas nodded. "Yeah. She never looked at me as trouble or John Doe, she looked at me as somebody's child. Your child. Little did I know at the time," Jonas paused and looked down. "About Mathew."

Eyes feeling, Cate choked up. "I am so grateful for her and Joe. More than I can ever say."

"She knows."

Grant's hand rested on the bag. "I see you got a new phone."

"Number is activated. I … I haven't turned it on yet," Jonas said. "I know I'm going to get bombarded with old texts and voicemails. I don't really know if I'm ready to see them yet or visit that life yet."

"Yet?" Grant asked. "So, you think you'll eventually go back?"

Jonas nodded. "I do. I have to, right? I mean, that's my life. My apartment. People I know. I can promise you both, I am going to do everything in my power not to get drawn back into the way I was. I learned a lot. But this here in William's Peak is Chip Doe's life."

"Aren't you one and the same?" Grant asked.

"Dad, I don't know anything. I just know it feels like I am fooling these people if I stay because I am not who they thought I was. I just still feel this pulling, like I'm searching for an answer and don't know the question."

Cate reached over and grabbed his hand. "You'll find it. I believe you'll find it." She glanced up when she saw Marge approach.

"I'm not interrupting, am I?" Marge asked.

"No, not at all," Grant answered.

"Chip, you have an hour free?" Marge asked. "I need to run to Fremont to that wine and spirits, they're the only place that carries the cordial juice and we need it for the chocolate covered cherries. You know how funny I feel about going there alone. I mean if you're busy ..."

"No, I'm not busy," Jonas replied and stood. "I'll go."

Marge looked at Cate then Grant. "Do you mind?"

Cate shook her head. "Not at all. We'll be in town."

Jonas leaned down, kissed his mother on the cheek, then his father. He swiped his phone bag from the table. "I'm ready."

Marge held out her hand. "After you, Chip. I got Joe's truck."

Cate kept the smile on her face, watching them walk away.

"What is it?" Grant asked. "What's on your mind?"

"She still calls him Chip. And he doesn't correct her."

"Maybe she's the only one who can convince him Chip and Jonas are one and the same."

"Maybe." Cate glanced back again, watching them get into the truck, then she returned to the conversation with Grant and her sandwich.

◆ ◆ ◆

It was a busy morning for Russ. Five traffic citations before noon and one of them was to Old Joe for careless driving. He kept stopping, going, jerking the car. He claimed he stepped on gum and his foot kept sticking the pedal.

Russ didn't see any gum, but he couldn't think of another reason Joe would be driving like that. He issued the citation but would probably just toss it out.

The station was quiet. Everyone was on patrol or out to lunch, which left Russ in charge of answering phones when they rang.

And they did.

"Williams Peak Police Department, Chief McKibben speaking. How can I help you?"

"Chief," the voice on the other line spoke. "This is Chief John Elliott over in Fremont. Glad I got you."

"John?" Russ sat down. "Wasn't expecting to hear from you."

"I wasn't expecting to call you. Thought our business was done."

"Me, too. What's going on?" Russ asked.

"Any chance I can get you to stop by today? Make the trip?"

"Sure. I'll head on up. Again, what's going on?"

"Well, Kevin McConnel our Guitar World pawn boy?"

"What about him?"

"Seems his mother found a gear bag in his room."

"I'm not sure what that is," Russ said.

"Usually, guitar players have them. They carry their cords, maybe a peddle, strings, stuff like that."

Russ snapped forward in his chair. "It belonged to our John Doe, didn't it?"

"Yep."

"Why didn't he sell it with the other stuff?"

"Ready for this?" John asked. "He didn't have the bag with the guitar. His mother saw him walking in the house with it two days ago."

"That gear bag would have been in the car with the guitar."

"He claims he went back to the site to see if he could find anything else and he found it then."

"A month later?" Russ said with disbelief.

John laughed. "We know that's not true, so because you got me started on this, I started looking, asking places he could have tried to sell it. It's a long story, but I just sent you a fax. It explains a lot. Take a look at the pictures and we can talk when you get here."

"Sounds good. Thank you. See you soon." Russ ended the call, and he was curious. He heard the whirling of the fax machine and walked across the station to it.

The second his eyes cast down to the emerging fax and he saw it, his mouth dropped open. "Well, I'll be."

He didn't need to look at the fax for long, he knew he had to get to Fremont and talk to the chief there.

Hurriedly, Russ grabbed an empty large envelope, placed the fax inside. He walked back over, grabbed the keys from his desk, and as he left the station, flipped the sign on the door to 'be right back'.

While getting in his car he saw the Truett parents across the street at the café. He paused in leaving and crossed the street.

"Afternoon folks," he greeted them. "Do you know where your son is right now?"

Grant asked. "Yes. Is everything alright?"

"Oh, yeah, actually great. Where is he?" Russ asked.

"He went with Marge to some liquor store in Fremont to get cordial juice or something," Grant replied.

"Even better. I'll call Marge to tell them not to leave. Thank you. Enjoy your lunch." Russ hurried away. He supposed he could have told them what was happening, but he felt Jonas had to be the one to know.

Jonas was right where Russ needed him to be.

Finally, Russ believed Jonas would get his answers and like Russ would finally close the chapter on the accident.

TWENTY-SEVEN

Jonas could have stayed at Guitar World all day, hours at least, but he knew Marge was anxious to get to the store and get that cordial juice. He was glad she stopped for him. It made his day.

The store was located on the main street of downtown, and they parked directly in front of it. A pull in spot, and Jonas could see the entrance.

Marge said she'd be right back, she always wanted to see what other juices they had so she could be a few minutes.

He was fine with that.

While sitting in the car, he put on the new protective case on the new phone, it was bulky and thick, and he didn't know if he liked it. Then finally drew up enough courage to turn it on.

As he expected the notifications popped up.

Four hundred text messages, sixty-three missed calls, and forty-two voicemails.

Marge wouldn't be in the store long enough for him to make a dent in those messages.

Perhaps that was his excuse to avoid checking them out, and Jonas slid the phone into his front tee-shirt pocket.

He was thinking about going into the store, but with his past, he wasn't quite certain he was ready to go into a liquor store to join Marge, even if she was getting stuff without alcohol.

Deciding he would check out his strings, he reached for the bag and that was when he saw three people run out of the store. It was worrisome running, like they were scared.

Curiously concerned, Jonas jumped from the truck and hurried into the store.

It was quiet, too quiet.

Marge was right there. As soon as he stepped in he saw her near the door holding two bottles of cordial liquid. She wasn't moving nor looking at the door. It was as if she was going to walk out and was busted, that was the look on her face.

Jonas started to laugh, ready to say, "Maw-Maw, what are you doing?" When he quickly noticed she was doing the same thing as the two cashiers and three other customers in line.

The manager's booth was against the far left wall and they all faced it.

Was there something on the news? He stepped toward Marge, reaching out.

"I said hurry up!" a man's voice yelled.

A quick look back to his left, Jonas saw it was a man, in a gray hoodie by the manager's booth.

His eyes went back to Jonas and that was when she saw him. Her face tensed up in a panic and mouthed the words, "Go. Get out."

She must have tried to run out like the others. So close to her escape, Jonas reached for her hand. He wasn't leaving her.

"And I told you!" the man's voice cracked as he shouted frantically and out of control. "No one move."

The man spun around with the gun in his hand. His arm extended; the gun aimed outward to point at Marge.

Jonas, without hesitation, dove in front of her as two consecutive shots were fired.

Both hit Jonas.

The impact sent the left part of his body back with the force of the hits and he fell into Marge before dropping to the floor on his injured side.

Everyone in the store screamed.

"Shut up!"

"Chip. Chip," Marge sobbed out.

Jonas felt one hand on his right arm, her other on his head.

"Get away from him!" the man yelled.

"No!" Marge blasted. "Chip, please."

He was stunned. Jonas could feel the sharp, burning pain, most of which came from his shoulder, he blinked several times to snap out of the shock.

Warm blood poured down his arm, he knew he had been hit in the shoulder, but there was an ache in his chest, like someone had punched him.

He had been there on the floor only a few seconds, but it felt like longer. Time moved in slow motion.

He brought this hand to his chest to check to see if he was bleeding and his hand hit his new cell phone. The phone he had placed in that thick bulky case, tumbled from his pocket, exposing the embedded bullet.

"I'm okay," he told Marge in a whisper. "I'm okay."

"Yeah, he's okay," the man snapped. "Get up. You're okay."

Jonas rolled onto his back to sit up some. When he saw his assailant. His mouth dropped open, and he instantly was breathless as he muttered in shock. "You."

Flash.

No longer was Jonas on the floor of that store, he was back in the car, after the accident.

"You're okay, you're okay. I have to undo your seatbelt," the passenger said.

Jonas released from the seat and dropped to the roof of the overturned car.

"I got you." He appeared at the window, reached down for Jonas' extended arms and pulled him out.

Once Jonas was out, he rolled on to his back to see him standing above him. He then looked over, saw the car and the small dancing flames on the car.

"We need to get you closer to help. Don't worry, I got you."

Then he reached down and lifted Jonas.

"You," Jonas repeated again from the floor then staggered to stand, never taking his eyes off the man with the gun.

The long hair was the same, beard a little longer, but there was no denying it.

The man robbing the store, the man with the gun ... he was the passenger.

◆ ◆ ◆

They hadn't even made it to Fremont when Russ called Marge. They were in Guitar World. He didn't tell her anything, just that he was headed to Fremont on business and not to leave until they met up.

Russ didn't expect the circumstances he faced when he arrived in the usually quiet town.

He had debated on taking his own car or the squad car. Opting for the squad car was a good thing, it gave him access when other cars were turned around at the blocked off street.

The younger officer leaned down to Russ' window. "What brings you to down here, sir?"

"Official police business, I see the chief is engaged already."

"Yes, sir. We have a hostage situation."

Russ nodded. Then he saw Old Joe's pickup truck. "Not the liquor store?"

"Yes, sir."

"I'm pulling over." Russ didn't wait for permission, he moved the squad car to the side, put it in park, and made his way to Chief John Elliott. "What's the situation?"

"Well, this was not how I expected to talk to you about this," John said. "We have hostages. Shots were fired. We aren't sure if anyone is hurt."

"I think two of my townspeople are in there."

"I don't know right now how many or who are hostages. I do know one thing. That's our guy."

"You're kidding me?"

John shook his head.

"I can tell you one thing I know. Our John Doe," Russ said. "Is in there, too."

◆ ◆ ◆

"David," Jonas said softly.

He stood off to the side of the window, peeking out. "What?"

"You told me your name was David."

The assailant, David looked turned with a growl. "They're out there. Is there another way out?" he asked the manager.

Nervously, she pointed. "Out back."

"You don't think the back door is covered, too?" Jonas asked.

With another shouting, 'shut up' he pointed the gun at Jonas. "There's no way out of here."

"Shut up!"

"You don't want to do this," Jonas said. "You don't."

"You don't know me."

"Your name is David. Look at me," Jonas pleaded. "You know me. I could never forget your face. A month ago. The accident."

David stumbled back some. "You lived?"

Jonas nodded. "I lived. Thank you. David, they're out there. Just put down the gun ..."

David growled loudly, almost a scream of fear and frustration. "I can't go back to jail!" He put the gun to his head.

"No!" Jonas screamed. "No! Don't! Don't do it. Let me help you."

"Help me? I shot you."

"You didn't mean to, you were scared. Let me help."

"Why would you want to help me?" David asked emotionally. "Huh? Why? I left you at that accident to die."

"No, you didn't. You pulled me out. You saved my life. You ... carried me. Carried me up a hill."

David shook his head. "I left. I left. I took your stuff and I left you there, and you're acting like I'm some kind of hero."

"You are."

"I was running from the cops," David lowered the gun.

"And you got in my car. Had you not, I would be dead. Dead. I wouldn't have a second chance at life. I wouldn't get to see I could live a better life. My parents would have lost a son. You saving me caused me to be saved, because I was bad. I was so bad. And you took nothing from me. You gave me life, hope, a chance at love and faith. Yeah, you did that."

"And you expect me just to surrender? To walk out of here?"

"Yes, I do," Jonas said. "With your head held high. And I will go to bat for you, Dude. I will do whatever it takes."

"They'll shoot me the moment I walk out there."

"Not if I walk out with you," Jonas said softly. "Give me the gun." He held out his hand. "Do the right thing. Take the first step to righting a wrong and to set you on a new path."

Confused, David shook his head. "What? What are you saying?"

"The words you said to me that night." Again, Jonas held out his hand. "Let's put down the gun and walk out of here together."

"We're coming out!" yelled the voice.

Russ' head jolted upward. "Jonas. That was Jonas," he said to John.

"John Doe?" The Fremont chief asked.

"Yes, that was his voice."

"Please don't shoot," shouted Jonas. "He's not armed. He's surrendering. I'm walking out with him."

"Hands in the air as you come out. Both of you!" yelled John.

"I can only raise one," Jonas replied. "I'm injured. We're coming out."

Russ cautiously stepped forward. Scared for Jonas because so many officers were there, all of them with their weapons raised. His eyes were focused on the door. It opened.

Russ felt his heart pound in his chest as he saw the man he had been looking for. He stepped out; hands raised. Right beside him was Jonas and he was covered in blood, only one arm lifted.

"Someone call an ambulance!" Russ shouted, charging forward.

He didn't care about the gunman; the other officers were quick to apprehend him. He ran to Jonas.

"You've been shot."

"I'm fine, Chief." Jonas peered up to him. "That was him."

"I know. Is Marge okay? Is ..." Russ didn't get to finish his question, Marge barreled out of the door and grabbed on to Jonas.

Marge was always a tower of strength, never wavering, yet she held onto Jonas with everything she was and she sobbed.

She said a lot, never stopped speaking through her tears. Russ couldn't understand a word she said, but he knew they had to be words of fear, gratitude and concern because Russ was feeling the same.

As far he could tell Jonas and Marge were alright.

At that moment, that was what mattered most.

TWENTY-EIGHT

They all raced to Fremont.

Once Joe received word, he went with Cate, Grant, Pastor Rick and Haley. They didn't have much information, other than Jonas was fine. He was shot and Marge was inconsolable.

Cate was the first through the emergency doors of the hospital and she feared the worst when she saw Marge. Her clothing had blood all over it and she was crying.

"Jonas," Cate whimpered.

"He's fine," Marge broke down. "He took a bullet for me. That man … he aimed at me and Jonas jumped in the way."

Cate's hand shot to her mouth.

"I'll never get over what he did for me. Never." Marge wept.

Grant and Cate stepped to her, but Joe grabbed a hold of her and held his wife.

Cate turned to Grant. "Our son did that. Oh, Grant, he did that."

"I know."

Haley's call of, "Chief!" caught their attention.

Russ stepped into the waiting room, holding up his hands. "Jonas is fine. They removed the bullet. They are going to admit him for observation. I know the police here want to talk to him. That boy … that boy has some powerful connections, I'll tell you." He looked at Pastor Rick. "He should have been dead … again."

Grant asked, "What? What do you mean?"

"I'll let him tell you. They said you can go back. He's in room seven …" barely finishing his sentence, everyone rushed by him.

Jonas adjusted himself to a more comfortable position. The wound actually hurt more since they took the bullet out. He had no more than some Tylenol. He didn't want more than that.

They had his arm in a sling, strapped to his chest, and he moved the contraption because it rubbed wrong.

"Jonas!"

He glanced up to the call of his name by his mother, not expecting to see an entire mob race into the room.

He smiled.

Cate grabbed his hand. "Are you alright?"

"I'm fine. Sore. But fine."

"Son." Grant put his hand on Jonas' leg. "Marge told us what you did. We are so proud of you. So proud you did that."

"It was nothing. Anyone would have done it." He looked over at Haley. "I got all my answers, Haley, all of them."

"The passenger," she said.

Jonas nodded.

"Boy," Joe spoke, looking at Russ. "You were relentless about this. That's why you were in Fremont."

"It all came together," Russ explained. "David Jenkins was arrested for selling stolen goods. Troopers in Iowa were bringing him in and he faked sick. They uncuffed him because they thought he was choking, and he took off. Got in your car, Jonas. He did end up injured. Trucker picked him up and brought him to Fremont. He left the hospital before they could ID him. He found Kevin on social media and worked out the guitar thing with him. He laid low while he healed, when he needed more money, he found Kevin again to see if he could sell your gear bag. On a hunch, the chief in this town asked around to see if he tried to sell it. He tried; the pawn shop wouldn't take it. They also brought your phone that was in the bag. We got footage. That's when they matched David."

"Wow." Jonas sat back. "You wanted to tell me all this."

Russ nodded. "They had him tracked to a motel out of town. They were gonna bring him in, but the robbery happened."

"I feel kind of bad," Joe said. "We had you believing Jesus was in the car with you, not some criminal."

"Oh, he was," Jonas replied with certainty. "He was just in the back seat watching it all unfold."

Pastor Rick spoke up. "We're glad that bullet missed anything vital."

"It almost didn't," Marge said. "He was shot twice. Once in the shoulder and once in the heart."

Amongst the confusion of voices, Jonas with a groan reached for the table next to him and held up his cell phone. "I will carry this with me the rest of my life to remind me how fortunate I am."

Haley took the phone, running her finger over the bullet. "This is your new phone."

"And I thought Dad was ridiculous when he paid all that money for that case," Jonas said. "That phone is also a sign. I never read the messages, that phone was a link to who I was. That phone tells me, that's gone. No looking back."

"Jonas?" Cate asked.

"I made up my mind, Mom." Jonas said. "After today, I know. Chip was always me. He was just the me I was afraid to be. I can't go back. I'm going to stay in Williams Peak."

Haley leapt forward to hug him, but as soon as she did, Jonas winced in pain.

"Sorry," she said.

"It's okay." He grabbed her hand. "Mom, Dad, are you okay with this?"

Grant smiled. "We're better than okay with this, Jonas. This is where you are supposed to be. Well, maybe not in the hospital. If you don't mind, can you try to stay out for a while?"

Jonas laughed. "I'll try. But while I'm healing, we need you in the worship band. I can't afford to lose you."

"I'll stay," Grant replied.

Jonas then looked at the chief. "I want to help David. Testify, help with legal fees, whatever, I want to help him. I need to."

Russ took a deep breath. "I don't understand. He's bad news."

"Maybe. But he can change. Anyone can," Jonas said. "I'm proof of that."

TWENTY-NINE

Three Years Later

Hand on the railing, Grant looked up the stairs in the living room. "Cate, come on."

"One minute," she replied.

"You only have one minute. I have to get to service and you are on coffee duty."

"It's supposed to be once a month," Cate said, coming down the stairs. "I swore I just did it two weeks ago."

"And if you did, who cares? Let's go. Truck's loaded. I need to get there."

"Maybe after the chief gets his coffee, I can get him to stay."

Grant laughed. "You've been trying since we moved here." He walked to the door and opened it. "If he hasn't in three years, he isn't."

"Doesn't hurt to ask."

"No, it doesn't."

"He listens outside, you know."

"I'm sure he does."

They stepped outside and Grant pulled the door closed.

He didn't lock it.

He hadn't locked his doors since they moved to Williams Peak, it was nice.

The decision to move there wasn't because of Jonas, it was all Grant. He would have made that decision regardless. The town and the people there did as much for him as they did Jonas.

It took a lot of convincing to get Cate to agree, she did, once

Jessie said she was fine with it.

Six months later, Grant took an early pension from the community college and ended up teaching history at Fremont High School. It was a commute, but there was little traffic on the straight shot, highway drive.

He wasn't ever giving up what he gained in Fremont, and the decision allowed him to watch Jonas grow even more. His relationship with his son was one he had always wished for.

He watched his son work two jobs, run the worship band, stay sober and get married.

Everyone saw it coming, no one was shocked when he and Haley wed.

Life in Williams Peak was simple. No surprises, Grant liked that.

So did Cate.

They had their routine and stuck to it.

Grant could hear the band warming up when he arrived. He knew he was late again, but not that late.

Leaving Cate in the back with the coffee social, Grant walked into the main body of the church.

The sound of fast rolling wheels caught his attention and he smiled when the baby, arms waving excitedly raced his way in the walker.

"There's my little buddy," Grant reached down. "Come to Pap."

"Dad," Jonas called from the stage. "Don't lift him he won't let you put him down. We have to run through these songs."

"Fine." Grant kissed the baby. "We'll play later, Chip," he said to the baby.

The baby squealed his dismay when Grant walked from him.

"See," Jonas said. "Look what you did. Now he'll cry all through practice."

Grant just smiled.

Finally, Cate thought, the coffee social was over.

She handed the cheese curl travel mug to Russ. "Here you go, Chief. Don't suppose since you're so late, I can convince you to stay."

"You ask all the time and I always say no, but ..." he lifted his hand. "I will be staying today."

"What?" Cate asked shocked. "You're joking?"

"No, I'm not. Someone asked if I would walk into church with them. I said I would. In fact, can you save a couple seats up front?"

"Absolutely. I'll see you there."

Cate rushed through pushing the tables aside. She was certain it had to be Jessie that was coming to service. She had just seen her the week before so it would be a really nice surprise.

She stopped by the nursery to peek in on Chip. She didn't want the baby to see her, because he would get fussy. Haley was handling it and Cate just went back to the church.

She took her usual seat in the front left row, said her hellos to everyone.

Haley came to the row a few minutes later, sitting next to her.

"Is the baby good?" Cate asked.

"Oh, he's fine."

"Hey, can you scoot down? The Chief asked that we save two seats. He's coming in with someone."

"The chief is coming to service? Wow. I wonder who he's bringing."

"I think it's Jessie."

"Oh, that would be nice."

The church lights lowered, and the colorful stage lights brightened as the screen lit up with the words, the band started playing.

Jonas had taken the band and the service to an entire new level. Pastor Rick was known as the cool, hip pastor and people came from miles away. The service was always packed, and the energy was magical.

Cate kept looking over her shoulder during the first song,

waiting to see the chief and Jessie.

It wasn't until the second song the Chief came in. His presence was noticed by everyone who knew him. Like he was a celebrity walking in.

But he didn't walk in with Jessie.

It was David Jenkins.

Cate wasn't angry when she saw him, she was happy.

From the moment he was arrested in Fremont, Jonas took his side.

He testified for him with the judge.

Cate and Grant helped as well. Had he not been in the car with Jonas, they would have lost their son that night. They did what they could for him. David didn't know they helped with his attorney's fees or money on his prison book. All he knew was they kept him in their prayers daily.

Instead of condemning him, many people in Williams Peak wanted to help him. It was a community thing.

Marge forgave him for that day and convinced Pastor Rick to start a bible study at the prison.

It took a year, but David finally joined.

Jonas kept his word. He wrote to David, visited him and spoke on the phone. He saw something in David and believed in him. In return, David started believing in himself.

Seeing him was a surprise. She knew he was up for parole; Jonas had given a statement to the parole board.

Cate hadn't heard a decision about it until he showed up in church.

David had changed. It was evident in the way he looked and walked.

He had weight on him, his hair was short, he looked happy and peaceful.

Cate knew when he slipped into the row he was anxious, she could tell. She grabbed his hand, kissed him on the cheek, and held on to him as they stood during the song.

It didn't take Jonas long at all to see him.

His face lit up and he grinned widely upon seeing David. For a second he stopped playing to point at him, give a thumbs up to show him in some way how happy he was to see him.

Shoulder to shoulder with him, Cate felt him breathe in deeply and slowly let it out. His arm was tense as she held on to it. He was uncomfortable, nervous. Of course, he would be. Fresh out of prison, starting a new life. He couldn't have picked a better place than Williams Peak.

It had a spirit about it that was contagious. He would learn soon enough.

To her, David would always have a place in Williams Peak, with her family and in her heart.

He saved her son's life in more ways than one, she would always be grateful he was the passenger in the car, that fateful, life changing night.

<><>END<><>

FROM THE AUTHOR

Thank you so much for reading this novel, I hope you enjoyed it.

Please visit my website www.jacquelinedruga.com and sign up for my mailing list for updates, freebies, new releases and give-aways. And, don't forget my Kindle club!

Your support is invaluable to me. I welcome and respond to your feedback. Please feel free to email me at Jacqueline@ jacquelinedruga.com

Printed in Great Britain
by Amazon